POLO, ANYONE?

POLO, ANYONE?

A NICK POLO MYSTERY

Jerry Kennealy

ST. MARTIN'S PRESS
NEW YORK

Library of Congress Cataloging-in-Publication Data

Kennealy, Jerry.
    Polo, anyone? / by Jerry Kennealy.
    p. cm.
    ISBN 0-312-01491-0 : $15.95
    I. Title.
PS3561.E4246P58 1988   87-29924
813'.54—dc 19   CIP

First Edition

10 9 8 7 6 5 4 3 2 1

For my sons,
Frank and Steve

POLO, ANYONE?

1

"Ron Dettman is rich, young, brilliant. Married to a gorgeous, sweet woman. In short, he's got everything going for him. But he cheats at poker, Mr. Polo. Why? That's what I want you to find out."

"You're sure he cheats?" I asked.

Paul Randall leaned back in his chair and tapped the tips of his fingers together. "Reasonably sure. I've never been able to spot it, but he . . . had a little too much to drink one night and let it slip out to someone. That's why I'd like to hire you. I was told that you are an expert when it comes to . . ." Randall paused, groping for the right words, "games of chance."

"Who told you that?"

He mentioned the name of an attorney I had done a few jobs for.

Randall was one of those men who could pass for anywhere between his late forties and early sixties, depending on how the light hit him. He was tall, thin, his thick, graying hair styled in the short, neat manner you'd expect a banker to have. His face was very bland; with regular features that could show either grief or joy with a minimum of effort. His eyes were like licked stones. He swiveled in his chair so that he was looking out his office window. I couldn't blame him. The view took in the whole Bay panorama, from the Golden Gate Bridge, past Alcatraz, the Bay Bridge, and over to the East Bay hills. It was a clear, brilliant day, the kind photographers love and tourists drool over—until the chilling winds that blow all the clouds and smog down to San Jose come in and start biting into their bones.

"We play once a week," Randall said. "Myself, Ron, some friends. The stakes can get pretty high. Last week Ron walked away with six thousand dollars."

"Do any of the other players suspect he's cheating?"

"I don't think so. Ron's always been lucky. At everything. And it's just lately that he's become a big winner. We play draw poker, and five- and seven-card stud. No wild cards, no low cards wild, nothing like that. Real poker. The other players are all professional people: attorneys, a doctor, a stockbroker, businessmen."

"Any chance one of the other players is in on the scam with Dettman?"

Randall swiveled his chair back. He looked shocked. "Certainly not. Why do you ask?"

"It's a lot easier when there are two cheats in a game. What about the cards? Who supplies them?"

Randall's desk was walnut and of a size that could accommodate a small helicopter. He reached into a drawer, took out a pack of blue Bicycle playing cards and passed them over to me. "These are the cards we used at the last game. My club supplies them. We always start with a fresh deck."

I riffled the deck several times. With Bicycles, the easiest way to mark them is to block out, or color, a portion of the small eight-petaled flower design in the corner of each card. I felt the edges. They were smooth and regular. "Do you always use this same brand of cards?"

Randall nodded his head. "I've been playing cards at the Sequoia Club for twenty years. We've always used the same brand cards."

"Always blue? Or do you use a red deck, too?"

"We use both."

"Ever change the deck during the game?"

Randall leaned back and considered the question for a good minute. "No, I can't recall ever changing the deck. Until now, I never thought there would be a reason to do so."

I riffled the deck once more. "These look clean, but I'd like to take them with me and check them out thoroughly."

"Certainly. Then you agree to help me on this?"

"When's your next game?"

"Tomorrow night." Randall opened a wooden humidor edged in silver and offered me a cigar. I passed and waited while he went through the routine of clipping off the end and lighting up with a slim gold lighter. "There's the matter of your fee," he said.

"What are the betting limits?"

"None, really, but we seldom bet more than a hundred at a call, though lately there have been bets as high as a thousand."

"Do you bet with cash or chips?"

"Chips, of course." He sounded a little offended.

"Do you want me to let you know if your friend is cheating, or do you want me to do something about it?"

He exhaled a cloud of smoke and appraised me through the haze. "Do something about it? I'm not sure what you mean."

"Do you want me to expose him right there? Or let him get away with it? Or just take him?"

Randall remained confused. "Take him?"

"If Dettman is cheating, I can get him into a big hand. He'll have cards he can't lose with. But he will lose. I'll win. He'll know he's been cheated. But he'll also know that I know he was, so there won't be anything he can do about it."

"You can actually do that?" Randall asked skeptically.

"Yes. For five hundred dollars up front, and any money I take from Dettman on the last hand."

Randall's face set into a serious *I can't approve that loan* look.

I gave him my best smile. "If you don't hurt Dettman, stick it to him good, he'll just go on cheating."

"All right. If you can do it, then do it." Randall got up and began pacing the room. "The poker problem is not my main concern, Mr. Polo. If Ron is cheating, I want it stopped, of course. But I also want to know why. If it's just a game, an ego problem, that's one thing. But if there's more to it, I want to know. I, that is my bank, has loaned Mr. Dettman's company a great deal of money." He stopped his pacing long enough to stare at me. "A great deal of money. There's no reason to suspect that there is anything wrong with his company. Even in the topsy-turvy world of high technology, Dettman Industries has never had any real problems. Ron is an absolute genius at what he does. That's why I never paid much attention to his big poker winnings. So do whatever you have to do. But I wouldn't want him exposed to the other players. I want it kept just between us."

"Just get me into the game, get me a seat right next to you. On your left. And I'll need to be staked, to enough money to stay in the game."

"Certainly." He tapped the cigar ashes over a big glass ashtray and his voice became assertive. "I'll stake you to all the money you need; however, any monies won during the game, other than what you make from Ron on the last hand and your five-hundred-dollar fee, will be returned. Agreed?"

"Certainly." I stood up and extended my hand. "And speaking of the five hundred, a check will be fine."

He studied me for a moment, then went back to his desk and wrote out the check. If you think bankers look sad when they lend you the bank's money, you should see them when it's their own. We discussed the time and place for our meeting tomorrow, then I rode the elevator down to the bank's lobby.

The teller was a cute, fresh-faced young woman who was at first reluctant to cash the check because I didn't have an account with them. She changed her mind when she saw Randall's name printed boldly on the check's upper left-hand corner.

2

I spent two hours in the San Francisco Business Library the next morning, researching Ronald Dettman. *Forbes* and *Fortune* had several articles on him. He was called a boy genius in his early career, a title that didn't seem to bother him at all. He was one of those bright young men with a garageful of wires, transistors, and superglue who came up with a revolutionary computer-programming device, started his own company, and in a few years had a hundred people working for him. Now Dettman Industries had grown into a national firm, with a plant in the Silicone Valley covering several acres and manufacturing branches in Georgia and Tennessee. His main contracts were with the government: satellites, sophisticated weaponry, but he also went after the home market with computer games and talking space toys.

The first picture I found of Dettman was taken twelve years ago, when he was in his mid-twenties. As the articles got newer, and Dettman got older, his hairline receded and his waistline expanded. He was wearing what looked to be expensive suits, spoiled by big, floppy bow ties.

That afternoon I went over the deck of cards Paul Randall had given me. They were clean: no daub marks, no pinholes, nothing obvious. And since Dettman was some kind of a genius, I even looked at them under ultraviolet light.

I made a trip to a store on Clement Street that sold all kinds of magic tricks and picked up a red and a blue deck of marked Bicycle cards, which had a disclaimer boldly printed on the package: "Marked Cards for Magicians. For magical purposes only. Not to be used in violation of any local, state, or federal laws."

I went home and practiced shuffling through the decks, making sure I could spot the markings, which stood out almost like neon if you knew what to look for, then spent a solid hour practicing false cuts, dealing from the bottom and center. At first my fingers felt like oversized sausages, but gradually the cards started flying out of the deck at a speed I was sure would fool any amateurs. If there were any professional gamblers in the game, I'd be in serious trouble.

By six that night I was waiting for Randall at Montgomery and California, dressed in a dark suit, white shirt, solid gray tie, and polished wing tips, my hair trimmed and conservatively brushed and a pair of clear-lensed glasses resting on my nose.

Not exactly a "multiple trickster of disguises" outfit, as one of my competitors advertises in the Yellow Pages, but Clark Kent had gotten away with it for years, and when Paul Randall's long, dark Cadillac pulled to the curb, he didn't recognize me at first when I tapped on his window.

"You all set?" Randall asked as I climbed in the back-seat. He sounded nervous.

The chauffeur smoothly guided the car into the late-evening traffic. The glass partition separating the spacious rear area from the front seat was closed.

"All set. I'll need a name. Why don't you call me Walker. George Walker. From New York City. I can be a venture-capitalist broker."

"Do you think you can pull that off if anyone starts questioning you?"

"I think so. If it gets too heavy, you can jump in and help me out."

Randall was smoking another of his big cigars. He blew a smoke ring that wobbled through the air and broke apart against the glass partition.

"I must confess I'm having second thoughts about this, Polo. I just can't understand why Ron Dettman would be cheating at cards."

"Who was it that told you he was cheating?"

"It doesn't matter," he said gruffly.

"I'll tap your foot when I'm ready to make my move," I said, "then I'll tap it again. When you get the second tap, no matter what card you're holding, no matter what the bets have been, and they will probably get pretty heavy, drop out of the game. Whatever money is in the pot, with the exception of what Dettman and I bet against each other after you drop out, you'll get back."

I could see he didn't like it, but he agreed, and the rest of the ride, not more than a few minutes, was in silence as we bumpered-to-bumpered up California Street alongside the cable cars, through Chinatown and up to the brick-paved entrance to the Sequoia Club.

Randall's driver, a small, spare man dressed in a dark suit and one of those silly chauffeur caps, jumped out and had the back door opened almost before the engine stopped turning over.

I'd never been in the Sequoia Club, but it looked much as I had expected it to, something out of an old Sherlock Holmes flick, with heavily polished wood paneling and beamed ceilings.

I followed Randall up a beautiful eight-foot-wide carved mahogany staircase, the steps carpeted in green-and-black plaid, to the second floor. Randall stopped and greeted several members, introduced me to a couple, never stumbling over the George Walker name. We finally made it to the club's game room. There were over a dozen round tables, all neatly circled with wooden captain's chairs. The tabletops were covered with green felt. There were a few card games in progress. Two of the tables were devoted to dominoes.

Randall steered me over to a table at the far end of the room. Three men were sitting there, nursing drinks. Dettman wasn't one of them. Randall made the proper introductions.

"Hope you don't mind some fresh blood tonight, gentlemen. This is George Walker. From New York."

"I don't mind fresh blood, as long as he's got fresh money," laughed a round-faced, balding man in his sixties. He had a thick English accent and was wearing a dark, double-breasted blue blazer and a yellow pocket handkerchief that matched his tie.

I got their first names down pat. Charlie, the English

9

chap, Al, a slightly Oriental-looking attorney, and Paul, a heavyset redhead who, when he claimed he was retired, got a few chuckles from the other men.

Randall snapped his fingers and a steward magically appeared. We ordered drinks; vodka martini for him, Scotch for me.

I got through ten minutes of small talk with no problem. Ron Dettman finally arrived and the game began. Chips were set out: whites twenty-five dollars, reds fifty, and blues a hundred. We all started with twenty-five hundred dollars' worth. The first few hands were unspectacular, small pots, winners raking the pot in with no more than a high pair.

I studied Dettman. He looked exactly as he had in the magazine pictures, and was still wearing one of those floppy bow ties. This one was polka-dotted. I've never seen anyone, even Cary Grant, look good in a bow tie, unless it was teamed up with a tuxedo. Dettman was outgoing, telling a few jokes as we waited in between hands.

Everyone at the table smoked, so I accepted one of Randall's cigars in self-defense. As the game went along, the bets got bolder, the pots higher. After an hour I found that Ron Dettman wasn't the only cheat at the table. Al, the attorney, shorted the pot every third hand or so, tossing in a chip short on raises, or taking out more than he put in. In the hour I figured, he shorted the pot by over a hundred bucks.

None of the other players were aware of it, and since Al was an attorney, no doubt he didn't think of it as cheating, just payment for the occasional legal question he was asked during the game.

Ah, but Dettman, he was a little more clever. He

had fast hands, no doubt from soldering all those tiny wires in his computers. He didn't have to be too fast for this group, though. I thought he'd be pulling something exotic, with marked cards visible only through special glasses, or little microchips of some kind imbedded in them, but he cheated the easiest way possible, the same way I used to when playing strip poker with Wanda Daily in the eighth grade. All he did was borrow a card from the deck now and then, usually an ace, sometimes a king or queen. He'd either save the card from the last hand he held, or he'd cull one from the discards.

Simple, really. All you have to do is palm the card and drop it in your lap, or slip it under your fanny. If someone else notices something's wrong with the deck, you just slide the card to the floor, as far away from your own seat as possible. Who knows how it got there? Nice and easy.

Dettman started winning more pots as the game went on and the drinks began to flow. The other players made it easier for him by doing what amateurs usually do, stay in the game too long, just to see one more card. I was wondering if there was some way I could get Randall to invite me in the game as a regular player every week. I'd never have to try to make a living as a private investigator again. These men may have been tops in their prospective fields, but in a poker game they were simply fish waiting for the hook. Of course, as long as they played among themselves, and didn't cheat, they'd never lose, or win, a lot of money, unless Lady Luck was with them that particular night.

I had made an occasional blunder just so Dettman wouldn't worry about the "new blood" in the game.

11

A steward brought a tray of hors d'oeuvres, and I used the break to go to the men's room and arrange the deck of marked cards in the order I wanted.

I waited until Dettman culled another ace, then, when it was my deal, I chose seven-card stud. I switched decks, then tapped Randall's foot. The cards went out smoothly. I dealt Dettman the following three cards: ace of diamonds down, four of clubs down, ace of hearts up. With the ace of spades sitting on his lap, it would be hard for him to keep a smile off his face, but I had to give him credit, he held it down pretty good.

I had a two and three of hearts down and the four of hearts showing.

"Ace high bets," I said.

"Well, let's heat the action up a little bit," Dettman said, throwing in a hundred-dollar chip.

Everyone covered the hundred but Randall, who had a king of diamonds showing, and upped it a hundred.

I dealt the next round of cards. Dettman got the four of spades. Al, the attorney, ended up with two tens showing. All his luck, I had nothing to do with that. He bet two hundred. Randall bumped it up another two hundred. Again, poker players rushed in where fools fear to tread, and everyone stayed in the game.

The next hand, Dettman got the ace of clubs. His eyes were dancing behind his thick-lensed glasses, but he didn't say anything, just took a long pull on his drink, then threw in two hundred dollars' worth of chips. Randall, who got another king to match his first one, promptly upped the bid by five hundred. I now had a six of hearts to go along with the four showing, with a useless jack of diamonds sitting in between them.

12

There was that feeling of undeniable tension in the room now, that feeling that came along every so often when everyone at the table knows that something big is going to happen. You can feel, almost taste, the tension. The world closes slowly around you, seconds stretch out, small noises become explosions. It was one of the reasons I'd been addicted to cards ever since my father taught me how to play cassino as a little boy. Of course I couldn't really enjoy it that much now, because I knew just what was going to happen.

No one improved his hand on the next round of cards.

"Pair of aces bets," I said unnecessarily.

Paul and Charlie finally folded. Reading the back of Al's cards, I could see he had three tens. Normally not a bad hand. But not this time.

Dettman looked at the three of us. He could understand Randall and Al hanging in there, but what the hell was I up to? But he had no worries. Four aces. The hand of a lifetime.

Dettman said, "I'll bet a thousand."

Al got the message and dropped out. Randall fidgeted briefly, then turned to Charlie, the now red-faced Englishman. "I'm about out of chips. Charles, why don't you keep tabs so we don't have to start dropping markers into the pot. I'll match the thousand and raise it a thousand." There was a chorus of gasps from around the table. My "I'll call" almost went unheard.

It was just the three of us now. "Last card down and dirty," I said, slowly slapping the cards down on the table.

Dettman picked his up with a steady hand. He

13

turned to Randall and said, "You going to stay in the pot, Paul?"

As all eyes turned to Randall, Dettman calmly switched the ace on his lap for the harmless six of diamonds I'd just dealt him.

Randall made a rolling gesture with his hand, inviting Dettman to get on with it.

"Okay," Dettman said. "Another two thousand."

I tapped Randall on the foot again. He frowned, studied his cards, then flipped them into the middle of the table. His voice was almost a croak. "I'm out."

"Call and raise another two thousand," I said. Dettman's eyes swiveled to me now, a look of uncertainty came over his features. He looked down at my cards. I could read his mind. What's this asshole up to?

"Nothing personal," Dettman said matter-of-factly, "but are you good for your bets? I mean, I don't know—"

"I'll back Mr. Walker's bets, if you consider that necessary, Ron," Randall said hotly. "He is my guest."

"No offense meant, gentlemen," Dettman said, the smile he was holding back for the whole hand breaking out now. "I cover the raise and bump it ten thousand dollars." He flashed a smile as hard as a car grille.

"If that's too high for you, Mr. Walker, I'll gladly lower it to whatever you think is reasonable."

"I'll just call. No sense in raising it any higher, is there, Mr. Dettman? The point has been made." I put on what I hoped was a really smug look and kept my eyes on his as I started flipping over my cards. "A straight flush, all hearts, two through six. Even if by some miracle you managed to pull a fourth ace out of your lap, it wouldn't beat my little straight flush, would it?"

14

Dettman's face, which had almost been the color of my cards, turned white at the mention of an ace on his lap.

"But, but that's impossible, you must have . . ."

He suddenly burst out of his chair, panting like a dog on hot day. I gave him a smile, then a wink, and reached out and started raking in the chips and the discards. I was more concerned with the cards, and as I pulled them together asked good old Charlie, "I lost track of the wagers. Just how much was the final betting?"

While Charlie was totaling up the amount, I quickly shuffled the deck, then, even quicker, switched it for the deck we had been using earlier, and which was now in my left-hand coat pocket. I suddenly remembered a story about an old-time San Francisco gambler, Shifty Jack Welz. Welz was fleecing a boatload of out-of-town gamblers in the basement of a jazz joint in Chinatown. Shifty was a perfectionist. The gaff had gone down perfectly; the money was in his pocket. All he had to do was switch the marked deck, lose a couple of small hands, and exit with the cash. Shifty went to the wrong pocket and when he passed the deck, the cards were suddenly blue instead of red. It was the end of a colorful career.

My switch went perfectly. Everyone was either looking at Charlie's little gold pencil scribbling up my winnings or at Ron Dettman, onetime boy wonder, who was stomping out toward the bar.

Charlie passed me a sheet of paper, which showed that Dettman was in to me for exactly fourteen thousand in notes. I didn't bother with what was in the pot. Randall was going to get all of that. I wondered how, or if, he was going to return the other players' losses to them.

15

Being a good winner, I offered to buy a round of drinks. Everyone declined except Charlie and Al, the attorney.

"Fantastic show," Charlie said. "What unbelievable luck. I wonder what the odds are on one player coming up with a straight flush and another with at least three aces in his hand? He had to have at least three. Do you think he had a fourth?"

"I had a hunch he did, or he wouldn't have pushed the betting that far. But we'll never know, will we?"

Charlie looked at me suspiciously over the rim of his glass. "Really unbelievable luck." He paused. "Wasn't it?"

Al took a quick sip of his drink, then picked up the deck of cards. "Unbelievable is right."

Dettman had departed for places unknown. Randall was looking solemn as we said our good nights. In the safety and quiet of the back of his limousine, he said, "That was awful. Are you absolutely positive he was cheating?"

"Yes. He was culling cards from the deck. Usually aces. Dropped them in his lap, and pulled them out when he needed them." I also told him about Al, the attorney, stiffing the pot.

Randall put his banker's voice back on, and we went over the details of the last pot again. I handed over the money I'd taken from him and his pals, which left me with the fourteen thousand owed by dear old Ron Dettman.

"Just how am I going to collect from Dettman?"

"I'm sure there won't be a problem." He took out one of his business cards and wrote down Dettman's office

16

number. "Call him in the morning. Where can I drop you, Mr. Polo?"

Off the Golden Gate Bridge if he had the chance, I thought. "Anywhere in North Beach will be fine."

He slid back the glass partition and gave instructions to the driver. Luckily we were only a few blocks away. I'd done my dirty job; now Randall wanted to get as far away from me as possible, as soon as possible.

3

San Francisco isn't much of a nighttime city anymore. The sidewalks roll up almost as early as they do in Des Moines. It was a little past eleven when Randall's chauffeur dropped me at the corner of Broadway and Columbus. I strolled down the block to Little Joe's restaurant, had one of the small booths all to myself, and ordered a veal sauté with pasta on the side. Cheating always made me hungry. And thirsty, so I ordered a bottle of Chianti.

For a guy who had just made over fourteen thousand dollars for a day's work, I was feeling pretty glum. There was something sordid, unclean about the whole affair. Still, Dettman had been systematically cheating people who regarded him as a friend, or at least a reliable business associate, and the fourteen thousand would be just a drop in the bucket to him.

The wine had just arrived when Ronald Dettman slid into the booth alongside me.

"What do I call you?" he asked. "Nick the Greek? I have a feeling that Walker isn't your real name."

"Did you follow me all the way over here to ask questions, or pay me off?" I signaled the waiter for another glass.

"How long have you known Paul Randall?"

I poured him a glass of the Chianti. "Cheers."

He didn't touch his glass. "You claim you're a venture capitalist. Tell me a little about your company. I may be able to throw some work your way."

"'Venture capitalist' is just another name for a gambler, surely you know that, Mr. Dettman."

"Ron, call me Ron," he said, reaching for his wineglass, then knocking down half the drink in one gulp. He was sweating heavily and used a napkin to wipe his forehead. "I'm not kidding about getting you some work, Mr.—Walker. Meet me at my office tomorrow. Around eleven. We can talk and have lunch."

"And you can pay me the fourteen thousand."

He rose, somewhat unsteadily, to his feet. "Yes, that's right. I rather imagine you'd prefer cash, wouldn't you?" He stared down at me, as if committing my face to memory, then stalked out of the restaurant.

Dettman Industries was located in Sunnyvale, in the heart of the Silicone Valley, some forty miles, and a forty-dollar-plus cab ride, from San Francisco. I had to take a cab. One look at my car and what little pretense I had as the redoubtable Mr. George Walker would be completely blown out of the water.

I was passed from the receptionist to a Mr. Hinkle, Dettman's "personal assistant," a casually dressed guy in

19

his early thirties, crowding five feet five. He apologized for Dettman, who had called saying he'd be a few minutes late. Hinkle offered to give me a tour of the plant. It was impressive. There were six separate buildings, all two-story-high slab-concrete affairs separated by large expanses of well-maintained lawn bordered with flowering pansies, petunias, and marigolds. There were a tennis court, swimming pool, and picnic areas sprinkled around the property.

The buildings themselves were bustling with activity, the most interesting being the "clean room," where workers dressed from head to toe in shiny aluminum-colored suits that looked like something out of an old science-fiction flick worked behind double-glassed windows.

"This is our wafer lab," Hinkle said. "The employees are working on the next-generation wafers, and the environment has to be absolutely dust-free. Have you done much investing in the high-tech area?"

My closest contact with wafers was with Nabisco, so I mumbled something that I hoped was an appropriate answer. "I'm just a money man. I match people with money. The technical end is a little beyond me." I looked at my watch pointedly.

Hinkle ignored it and took me for the rest of the tour. By the time we got back to the lobby, it was close to noon.

The receptionist handed Hinkle a piece of pink paper, which he read studiously, then turned to me with sad eyes. "I'm afraid Mr. Dettman won't be able to make it, sir. He's been unavoidably detained. He hopes you'll forgive him and come to his home this evening for cocktails at seven."

He wrote down Dettman's address on a blank piece of the pink notepaper. When Hinkle heard me asking the receptionist to call me a cab, he said, "Oh, that won't be necessary, sir. We'll have someone give you a ride wherever you're going."

"Someone" turned out to be a pleasant-faced, middle-aged guy named Don Pichel. He escorted me to a Peugeot diesel sedan, pointed it in the direction of San Francisco, and never once pushed the speedometer over fifty, which made it easy for the dark-blue Ford that stuck behind us for the whole trip.

Pichel started pointing out landmarks, giving what he thought was a friendly tour to an out-of-towner. I told him to drop me off near Union Square, and, when he got to the corner of Powell and Geary, I thanked him, jumped out, and dashed into the Geary Street entrance of Macy's.

A heavyset guy with a salt-and-pepper goatee jumped out of the blue Ford and followed me. I lost him somewhere between women's lingerie and the Bridal Shop, then hustled out the store's O'Farrell Street exit, hoofed it up Powell to where I could get a look at the blue Ford, which was parked next to a fire hydrant, and huddled in a doorway until the goateed gentleman came back. He shrugged his shoulders and turned his palms up in a helpless gesture and got back in the car.

I copied down the license plate and walked up Geary to Lefty O'Doul's, and, after wolfing down a roast beef sandwich, used the restaurant's phone to call the Department of Motor Vehicles in Sacramento. Now I know you've always seen TV and movie private eyes call up a buddy in the police department and have him run the plate for them. Fair enough, but there's another way. You just post a bond and open an account with Motor Vehicles. It's quick, easy, and, best of all, tax-deductible that way. The DMV clerk punched the right magic buttons, and within seconds read off the listed owner to the two-year-old Ford, California License 1KFK100. It belonged to a J. J. Murphy, with an address in San Jose. I knew who Murphy was, a retired Los Angeles policeman who got out of the job just slightly ahead of the grand jury's interest in him, moved up north, and started a rent-a-cop business; mostly uniformed security guards at shopping centers and industrial plants. I had met him once at an investigators' conference in San Diego. He no doubt ran security at Dettman Industries. There had been several uniformed guards in view during my tour. So Dettman was going through a lot of trouble to find out just who I really was. That didn't bother me. Much. What did bother me was whether or not he planned to fork over the fourteen thousand bucks.

4

I was going to hang on to the George Walker impersonation as long as possible. Not only out of loyalty to my client, but because I knew it was driving Dettman up the wall. This necessitated another cab ride. I arrived at Dettman's house at twenty after seven, fashionably late; I didn't want to look too greedy, and had the cabbie wait for me. It was a big house, three stories, all brick, ivy covering most of the surfaces. The window trim was painted a bright white. There was a small front lawn guarded by a neatly groomed privet hedge. The front door was oak trimmed in brightly polished brass.

The woman who answered the door was wearing a turquoise dress, bare at one shoulder, held together by just one button at the top of the covered shoulder. The color accented her soft blond hair and tanned skin. She looked to be in her early thirties and the dress didn't attempt to hide the fact that she had the same figure she had had when she was a high school cheerleader. It was something I would have bet on. The cheerleader. She looked the type.

"Hi," she smiled, showing crow's-feet at the corner of her eyes. She'd have to limit her sunbathing time pretty soon. "You must be Mr. Walker. Ronnie's told me all about you. Come in."

After she closed the door I followed her down the hallway. The floor was a light-colored parquet. Her heels clicked merrily as she led me into a larger room, the walls cream-colored, covered with dozens of oil paintings ranging from bold, colorful abstracts to what appeared to be a genuine Matisse and a couple of Dalis. The furniture was light, almost the color of the walls. She went over to a low table covered with liquor bottles, glasses, an ice bucket in the shape of a man's top hat, and small bowls of nuts and pretzels.

"You look like a bourbon man to me," she said, bending over the table, her hair falling in front of that lovely face.

I didn't protest as she poured a good three fingers of something brown from an unlabeled cut-glass decanter. She dropped a lone ice cube into the glass, handed it to me, then went back and fixed herself a drink. Hers was clear. The smell of gin permeated the air. It wasn't her first of the evening.

She extended a manicured hand. "I'm sorry. Where are my manners? I'm Alicia. Ron's wife."

I shook her hand, wondering if she had been waiting for me to kiss it instead. She sat down with a whoosh into one of the overstuffed easy chairs, almost spilling her drink.

I sipped at mine. It tasted like old, expensive bourbon.

24

"Where's Ron?" I asked.

She shook her head, causing the blond hair to swish back and forth. "He's running late again. He's always running late." She frowned, as if trying to remember something. "He said that if you got here before he did, that I was to give you that envelope."

She pointed her drink to a glass-topped table. The name "G. Walker" was printed in block letters on a manila envelope. I picked it up. It felt wonderfully heavy. The back had been sealed, then reopened and resealed. Had good old Ronnie left out a few dollars and, feeling guilty about it, reopened it and put in the proper amount? Or had his wife gotten curious? I wouldn't want to book a bet on those odds.

I slipped the envelope in my coat pocket. "I think this is all I'll need, Mrs. Dettman. I won't have to see Ron now."

"Don't you want to count it?"

"Count it?"

She leaned forward in her chair with some difficulty. "It's money, isn't it? Ronnie's always giving envelopes stuffed with money to people." She settled back into the chair and her lips formed a pout. "Always."

I took a healthy swig of the bourbon and put the glass down. "Just one hell of a guy, old Ronnie, but I do have to get going. Tell him if there are any problems, I'll be sure to get right back to him."

She got unsteadily to her feet. "Oh, don't go. He should be back any minute now. We're going out to dinner."

I made my apologies and threaded my way back to the front door. She followed me all the way, the drink in

her hand, spilling drops of gin all over that beautiful par-
queted floor.

The cab was waiting, the engine sighing quietly.
There was no sign of a dark blue Ford, and I counted the
money in the backseat while we headed back to North
Beach. I had the driver drop me off at Capp's Corner, a
restaurant just a half block from my flat. I dined well,
drank well, then got into a liar's dice game at the bar, and,
after dropping a hundred dollars, decided that all good
things must come to an end, and that maybe this lucky
streak of mine was over. Was that ever an underestima-
tion.

I walked up Green Street to my flat and was just
getting up the stairs when someone shoved something
into my back and told me not to move while he patted me
down. He took the envelope, then cracked me hard on
the back of my head. While I was going down he kicked
my feet out from under me. I fell like an overweight pan-
cake to the sidewalk, landing with a splat as the back of
my head met concrete.

He leaned over and placed the barrel of a revolver
right between my eyes. He had a large pitted nose and a
cold smile that showed jagged yellow teeth.

"I'm going to try and make this as painless as possible, pal. But if you struggle, I'm going to blow your fucking head off."

He kept the gun between my eyes. "Put your right
hand out straight. Palm up."

I hesitated and he shoved the gun barrel down into
my face. "Do it! Now!"

I moved my arm out, my eyes twisting to see what
he was up to. He straightened up, put his right foot on my
elbow and started to raise the left one up in the air.

"Don't struggle, pal, it won't hurt much. Not as much as a bullet. I just want to teach you a lesson about card dealing."

There was no way I was going to let him play Fred Astaire on my hand without putting up a fight, and I started to yell when suddenly the air was pierced by a loud whistle. A woman's voice started shouting, *"Polizia! Polizia!"*

The guy with the gun did what any normal mugger would do at a time like that. He started running.

I rolled over to my side and watched him skitter down Green Street and hop into a car. No dark blue Ford this time. It was silver. One of the General Motors clones; a Buick, Pontiac, or Chevrolet. I got to my feet in slow stages and started off after him, but it was never close. I tried to see his license plates, but all I saw was a blur of taillights as he turned the corner.

I walked up the hill in a slight stoop, like Groucho Marx when he was chasing a young blonde in a nurse's uniform. The only difference was that Groucho could have done some good when he caught up with his nursey. I certainly couldn't. I flopped down on the front stairs and looked up at the imposing figure of Mrs. Damonte. Mrs. Damonte is somewhere between eighty and a hundred and twenty. She has been the downstairs tenant since my parents first owned the flats. When my folks died, and I inherited the property, I didn't think it would be nice to ask the little lady to leave. That is, until I found out that she was paying a hundred and seventy-five bucks a month for a unit that could bring in fifteen hundred. I tried raising the rent fifty dollars and thought I had started World War III. Now she reluctantly handed me over two hundred a month, which doesn't even pay the taxes, but at least she hadn't poxed me with any Sicilian curses lately, and she does let me have my pick of what she grows in the garden.

Mrs. D had on her everyday long black dress. She was always dressed and ready to go to a funeral at a moment's notice. There was a large brass whistle hanging around her neck.

"That man. You know him?" she asked me in Italian.

"No. He was a robber. Thank you very much," I answered back. Mrs. D was about the only person I spoke Italian to since my parents died, and our conversations aren't exactly long and stimulating, so I find myself getting tongue-tied most of the time. "Did you call the police?"

"Nopa."

Nopa. That's about as close as she gets to speaking the English language, though she seems to understand it pretty well.

"Good," I said. "I don't think he'll be back." Not with the watchdog of North Beach stationed at her window.

The first thing I did when I was safely locked in my flat was hop in the shower. There was a small cut on the back of my scalp where he must have hit me with the gun. My suit coat had a tear in it, and the phony glasses were broken. No loss there; I wouldn't be needing them anymore. There was still a visible indentation between my eyes from the gun barrel. It was going to leave a goofy-looking bruise. I dressed quickly in slacks, a turtleneck sweater and jacket, and, after checking the streets from the front window, went out and down to the garage for my car.

28

I mentioned earlier that I couldn't drive my buggy down to Dettman's place because it would blow the George Walker cover. The car is a battered old Ford sedan, an odd shade of tan, the fenders bent a little, the doors with more dings than Buddy Rich's cymbals. There's a long whip antenna, one of those revolving red lights that can be stuck on the roof, and which I always leave visible on the front seat. I also have spotlights and what looks like a police radio but is actually nothing more than a microphone, the cord taped harmlessly under the dash. A few "Wanted" posters and hot-car sheets are spread around the seats. It looks exactly like an "unmarked" police car. It runs well and has a good AM-FM radio that, thanks to that long antenna, can bring in the few stations that aren't devoted to hard rock and country music. There's a tape deck hidden in the glove compartment, and a .38 snub-nosed revolver is stuffed inside the passenger's side headrest. All the comforts needed for living in the fast lane in the City by the Bay. Of course the car's real charm lies in the fact that I can park in red zones, white zones, in front of fire hydrants, and even on the sidewalk, and chances are fifty-fifty that I won't get a traffic tag. I wrestled the .38 from the headrest and headed back to Dettman's house.

5

I parked in front of a fire hydrant a block away from Dettman's house and killed the motor. The street was quiet,
the only sounds an occasional dog's bark.

I waited fifteen minutes, then got out of the car and
walked down the street. No silver General Motor specials,
nobody scrunched down behind the steering wheels of the
bevy of Hondas, BMWs, and Alfa-Romeos that littered
the block.

Dettman's wife answered the door almost as soon as
I'd rung the bell. She was still carrying a drink in one
hand.

"Oh, I thought it might be . . ." She squinted her
eyes and tried focusing in on me. The left one looked red
and puffy, as if it had been hit recently. "Aren't you . . ."

"Walker. We met earlier. Is your husband in?"

"No. He always calls if he's going to be late, but I
haven't heard from him." She took a sip of her drink. "Do
you know where he is?" she asked; then, before I could
reply, she said, "You look different."

"I could use one of those," I said, pointing at her glass. She staggered back, holding the door open for me. We went back to the room with the paintings. I kept close to her. She looked as if she would fall down any minute.

"Let me get that for you," I said, taking her glass and adding a small amount of gin. "Any idea where Ronnie might be?"

"No." She burped lightly, then turned her lips up at the corners and grinned, the way a little girl does when she's been caught trying on Mommy's makeup. "Well, actually, I do have an idea, but . . . he did come home for a few minutes, right after you left, but he said he had to go out again and . . . I think I had one too many drinks, Mr.——"

"Call me Nick. Sometimes you need one too many. I guess it's not easy being married to a guy like Ronnie. All those late business meetings."

"Yes, lots of those, damn it."

I made myself a light whiskey soda. She perched on the edge of the sofa and watched me, drained what was in her glass and handed it out to me. "Just a light freshening, please."

We had about five minutes of nonsensical small talk, and she asked me to freshen her drink one more time. Then the long blond hair fell in front of her face and her chin dropped to her chest, the drink to the carpet. I caught her before she slid onto the floor and put her on the sofa, with a pillow under her head.

I started checking through the rooms on the main floor. The kitchen was all white tile walls, dark oak cabinets, and butcher-block countertops. There was a large formal dining room, with a beautiful round black-lacquered table that could have comfortably held King

Arthur and most of his knights. At the rear of the house was what I imagine Dettman would call his library or home office. Three of the walls were nothing but bookcases jammed with everything from fine leather-bound editions to flaky-papered catalogs and paperbacks.

A massive oak desk with hand-carved legs stood in the center of the room. Three phones, one red, one white, the other blue, sat patriotically on one end of the desk. A big Xerox copy machine occupied one corner of the room; a card table, with a chess set and a wooden poker-chip carousel holding chips and decks of cards, was in the other corner. The wall without books was covered with pictures of Dettman on a golf course smiling back at the camera, either with his arms around a co-golfer, or waving a putter in the air. Paul Randall was in several of the photos. Two framed pictures showed Dettman and his wife in the winning circle at the racetrack, standing next to a beaming jockey and a proud-looking thoroughbred.

The center and left- and right-hand desk drawers of the desk were locked. The bottom drawers held nothing but envelopes and scratch pads.

I tiptoed back to Mrs. Dettman. She was still out, making light snoring sounds, her eyes squeezed shut, forehead corduroyed in thought, as if she was having a nightmare.

I tried the upstairs. There was one large room with overstuffed couches and chairs and one of those huge TVs, the screen covering almost an entire wall. Down the hall was a room, a good twenty feet square, that had been converted into a walk-in closet, with rows upon rows of coats, dresses, hats, and at least sixty pairs of shoes. There was a separate rack for leather clothing, one just for evening gowns, and so on.

Dettman had his own version next door. A little smaller, but the clothing was just as neatly laid out: a rack of business suits, at least a couple of dozen; Levi's and sport shirts; and, while good old Ronnie didn't have his wife's fetish for shoes, he wasn't going to have to go barefoot for the rest of his life.

There were two bathrooms, one definitely hers: pink tile, a sunken Jacuzzi, a makeup vanity littered with jars of cosmetics and perfumes. There was a large metal object that looked like a Danish-modern coffin at first glance. It turned out to be an ultraviolet tanning table.

Dettman's bathroom was smaller, but still big enough for the 49ers' offensive line to towel off in after a game. I was beginning to wonder if Ronnie and Alicia ever met anywhere other than in the hallways. The bedrooms were separated by a door that locked on both sides. Hers was all white and pink again, the walls covered with a glossy cream grasscloth. Pastel Impressionist paintings of Monet's gardens hung on the walls. The bed frame was brass, king-sized, a white canopy hanging over it.

Ron's room was done in dark browns, beiges, and orange. The walls had abstract paintings similar to the ones downstairs. The top of a dresser was cluttered with silver golfing trophies. One of the inscriptions read: "Ron Dettman, Club Champion, St. Francis Golf Course, 1986."

I rummaged through Dettman's dresser drawers; nothing much other than the usual supply of socks, underwear, pajamas, and dozens of those god-awful bow ties. In the nightstand next to the bed was a .38 revolver, a twin to the one in my pocket. I checked it. It was loaded. I emptied it and threw the bullets on the carpet. Maybe Dettman would come home late, trip on them and break a leg. The room had a deserted feeling about it. There wasn't a book, a Kleenex box, a coffee cup, or anything else there that looked as if a human being had used it lately.

I went back downstairs, took a blanket from a hall closet and draped it over the still-sleeping Alicia Dettman. She looked better now; the frown was gone. I tucked her in as best I could, then checked my watch, which showed it was almost one in the morning.

I went back to Dettman's office and tried the locked desk drawers again. They were tight. No way of springing them without leaving obvious marks. Up to now I could hardly be considered a burglar. I had been invited in. But if I tore Ronnie's desk apart, he no doubt would call the cops. Or would he? He was nervous enough to have me followed once, then have a goon, who looked as if he knew his job, beat me up. The thought of the beating got me hot again, so I examined the desk closely. The center-drawer lock was a Bixler spring type. Serious stuff. You turn the key and a shaft goes up above the drawer, makes contact and then opens up like an umbrella. The two side drawers had the same locks. Now in the movies, some guy, usually a Robert Wagner type, reaches into the inside pocket of his tailor-made tuxedo, takes out one skinny little piece of shiny metal, sticks it in the lock, wiggles it a few times, and presto, he's in. Looks good, but it just doesn't work that way. Any decent lock needs at least two picks, maybe three. I had a set of good picks at home, but even with those, a Bixler lock can drive you up the wall.

I got down on all fours and studied the desk from below. It was a solid piece of old-world craftsmanship.

Each piece cut by hand, planed down to fit perfectly. I suddenly smiled, remembering an old burglary case I had worked on, and got up so fast I hit my head, then made my way into the kitchen, picking up a can of olive oil and several knifes, starting with a thin paring knife, all the way up to a meat cleaver big enough to bring down a redwood tree.

I dipped the smallest knife into the olive oil and started working it in the tiny crack where the top of the desk met the frame. It was rough work, and I was sweating heavily by the time I got the top raised a fraction, enough to put in the next-thickest knife. I kept working all the way around the desk. By the time I got the meat cleaver in, the desk's dowels could be seen. No nails in this beautiful baby. I'd wipe olive oil on the dowels, then pry up. The top finally was up a good inch, enough for me to reach in and retract the Bixler lock shaft on all three top drawers. The two small drawers were disappointing: envelopes, various sizes of different-colored paper, erasers, paper clips. But the center drawer had an interesting surprise: some black-and-white glossies of myself and Dettman's man Hinkle strolling around his plant. There were a few close-ups of me and a piece of paper with J. J. Murphy's letterhead, a brief typed report saying that "the subject Walker has been positively identified as private investigator Nick Polo." My address on Green Street was printed right alongside a brief rundown of my time in the police department and my stint in federal prison.

J. J. Murphy had probably recognized me from the pictures. So Dettman had known who I was, probably since this afternoon.

There was an envelope with "Confidential" stamped

on it in bright red letters. I opened it. It contained a report with schematics of oddly shaped contraptions that could either be satellites, silicone chips, or the parts to a vacuum cleaner, and pages and pages of mathematical formulas, all of them well beyond anything I had picked up in high school algebra.

I took them over to the copy machine and ran off a set of prints, started to put the originals back in the drawer, then decided to keep them, along with the prints. I used a handkerchief to wipe off everything I'd touched, then went over to the poker-chip rack, shuffled through a deck of cards, came up with four aces, and put them in the middle of the center drawer. Then I lowered the desktop back down to its normal position.

The knives and olive oil went back to the kitchen, then I took one more look at the peaceful Mrs. Dettman and left.

6

I was up early the next morning. The first job of the day was to salt away the original and copies of the documents I had taken from Dettman's desk. My father was a brick-layer, which is why the flat looked somewhat like a Roman fort. He was also a master carpenter, and one of the best things he ever built was a little hideaway under the kitchen sink. There was a false back that opened up to reveal a nicely bricked little vault. He'd kept the family jewels, a few gold coins, and the best of his homemade grappa there. The jewels and the coins still rested in dusty purple velvet bags. The grappa was long gone. I put the copies into the vault, stuck the originals into an envelope, and by seven the next morning I was parked down the street from Dettman's house.

A few minutes past eight a battered old pickup, the back jammed full of lawnmowers, pulled up in front of the house. A large, heavyset woman in a white dress got out of the truck. The truck took off and the woman walked up to the front door and let herself in with a key.

I'd gone through a full thermos of coffee by nine-thirty and had nothing to show for it except a rumbling stomach and complaining kidneys.

A bright red Alfa convertible scooted out of the driveway just before ten o'clock. Alicia Dettman was behind the wheel, the blond hair tucked away under a black scarf.

I waited ten minutes more, then made my way to Dettman's front door. The lady in white answered the bell. She was in her mid-fifties, with jet-black hair and skin the color of darkened copper.

"Hi. Is Ron in?" I asked.

"No, sir. He's not home now," she said with a slight accent.

"How about Alicia?"

"You just missed her, sir. Can I tell them who called?"

"No, don't bother. I'll get ahold of Ron at the office."

I tried that. Dettman's secretary would tell me nothing other than that he was "unavailable." I got transferred to my tour guide of yesterday, Mr. Hinkle, and told him to relay the message to Dettman that Mr. Walker was very anxious to get ahold of him.

"Any special message?" Hinkle asked.

"Just tell him there are four more aces in his desk drawer at home." I hung up before Hinkle could ask any questions.

Paul Randall was at a meeting, according to his secretary. I wondered if he was bumping heads with Dettman somewhere.

That left me with time on my hands, a bump on my head, and a sour taste in my mouth.

I had a late breakfast, took a nap, then went back to the phone. Dettman and Randall were still unavailable. I then called J. J. Murphy Investigations and finally got someone who would talk to me. Old J. J. jumped at my offer.

"Mr. Murphy, I operate a small electronics firm and I'm afraid that one of my most trusted employees has been doing business with my competitors. You've come highly recommended, sir. I want this investigated, and money is no problem. I want you to handle the job personally."

Murphy went into a five-minute dissertation on how he'd handled many such investigations.

"Where can I meet you, Mr.——"

"Hartman," I said. "I don't want to meet you at my plant. There's no telling how many of our people are involved. Why don't we meet at, say, the Oasis, at six tonight."

Murphy readily agreed and gave me a description of himself so I'd be sure to recognize him.

The Oasis was a popular watering hole for the Silicone Valley crowd, and I was in the parking lot at five-thirty. A red Cadillac Eldorado pulled in just a few minutes before six, with J. J. himself behind the wheel. He sensibly parked in the rear of the lot, away from other cars, so no one would bang into his doors. His round, cherubic face was beaming as he jauntily walked into the bar. At six-forty he walked out a much less happy man. He had the Cad's door opened when I stuck the barrel of the .38 into his back.

"Don't make a move, J. J. Just stand still."

His slack body tightened. Gray hair stood up and away from over the dandruffed collar of his sport coat. I

39

gave him a quick frisk. The only thing he had other than the usual wallet and keys was a small plastic beeper. I put a black woolen scarf over his eyes, tying it tightly at the back of his head, and guided him into the car's front seat.

"All the money I have is in the wallet, buddy, if—"

"Shut up, or you're a dead man. Just sit there." I walked around the other side of the car and got in. "Now just quit blubbering and answer a few questions and you'll be on your way home in a few minutes, none the worse for wear." I poked the gun into his ribs to keep his attention.

"You had two men on a tail job yesterday in a blue Ford. Later you switched to another man in a silver job. Who were they?"

"I don't have any—"

I shoved the gun deeper into his ribs, then cocked the hammer. "J. J., I'm not here to fuck around. My client said to either get the information the easy way or to just waste you. If someone comes out of the bar and sees you with that scarf over your head, I'm going to get nervous and pull the trigger on this silenced gun that's pointing at your heart, so I'm not going to wait very long for my answers, baby."

That was all the prodding he needed. "I had two men on a simple tail job. They've both been with me for years, Dick Jones and Dan Dobbins."

"Yeah, we know all about them. It's the other guy we're interested in. Big man with bum teeth. He handled an assignment last night. Tried to do a rough-and-tumble job on a member of our organization."

"No, no. I don't have any—"

"Goddamn you, don't lie to me. One more time and I'll—"

40

There was suddenly a very ugly smell in the car. It didn't take long to figure out what it was. Poor old J. J. had lost control of his bodily functions.

"All right. Maybe he wasn't your man. But I've got a man at the far end of the lot with a rifle aimed at you right now. I'm going to leave now. If you try and make a move, even reach up and touch that scarf covering your eyes, in the next five minutes, you're a dead man. And J. J. I wouldn't tell anyone about this. Even your client. We've got him wired."

When I drove out of the lot a minute later, J. J. was still sitting there rigidly in his front seat, his lips moving, no doubt saying his prayers.

I stopped at the first bar I could find on El Camino Real. It was one of those Western jobs: sawdust on the floor, a jukebox full of Willie Nelson, Wayland Jennings, et al. The customers wore expensive denim pants and silk shirts with snaps instead of buttons. Pseudo shit-kickers. A small dance floor was jammed, the stomping of boots echoing over the music.

The bartender greeted me with a big "Howdy, partner." His shirt sleeves were rolled all the way up to his bulging biceps.

"Give me a Jack Daniels over." I laid a five-dollar bill on the bar. "I need some change for the pay phone."

When he brought my order, I asked, "Any way to turn the volume down on that hayseed music?"

His eyes widened momentarily, then he grinned. "You don't like C&W, boy, you came to the wrong place."

I scooped up my change and found the phone booth back by the men's room. I dialed my number, heard my answering machine's recorded message come on and punched in the code numbers so it would relay messages. There was just one, but it was a good one. Ron Dettman's voice, sounding mad as hell. "Call me right away at 555-4216."

I did so. The phone was answered by a woman with a soft, sexy voice.

"Mr. Dettman, please."

"Who's calling?"

"Tell him it's either George Walker or Nick Polo. He can take his pick."

Dettman must have been standing close by. He spoke almost immediately. "What the hell kind of a game are you playing, Polo?"

"Did you find those four aces, Ronnie?"

"What the fuck do you want?"

"First of all, I want back the money you had the gorilla take off me."

Dettman spoke in a metered tone, stressing each word. "You are in this over your head now, Mr. Polo. I suggest that you return that material to me right away. You don't know what you're dealing with. That is very confidential information."

"Then what were you doing leaving it around in a desk a Boy Scout could break into?"

"I want that material back. Right now!" he shouted.

The bartender seemed to have cranked the music up another ten decibels, so I had to squeeze one ear shut and jam the other into the receiver to hear Dettman. "This is getting us nowhere. I want that money back."

"You cheated me, you bastard!"

"No, I just outcheated you. Now are we going to

42

make a deal, or am I going to make copies of those diagrams and start peddling them down in the Valley?"

"All right. You'll get your money, but don't show those diagrams to anyone. Anyone at all, you understand, or you'll live to regret it."

"You try sending anybody after me again and you *won't* live to regret it. I'll call you in a couple of hours. Have the money ready."

I broke the connection before he could reply and made my way out of the bar. The bartender gave me a big wave. I could read his lips over the drone of the music. "So long, partner."

7

You call the telephone company office that handles your number, get connected to your service representative, then ask her pleasantly just who is listed for that certain number you're interested in. She will ask you in a very polite tone (they talk that way now that there is competition) if that number shows up on your bill. Since by now she already has your latest billing on the computer in front of her, she damn well knows it's not there. If you say no, you just want to know to whom the number belongs, she'll stiff you. But a simple little story like "No, it's not on the bill, but someone keeps calling and leaving that number on my answering machine and I want to know who it is" will induce the operator to give you the right information. If the number is listed. If it's not listed, you have to do it the hard way. Luckily the number Dettman had given me was listed. It belonged to a J. Drew, address 1777 Taylor Street, San Francisco.

I cruised by 1777 Taylor. It was a modern twenty-story apartment house sticking out of the side of Russian Hill. I parked and watched a couple of cars drive up to the front of the building. They were met by a big Irish-looking guy in gray slacks and a blue blazer. He used the phone in a glass-walled office before letting anyone enter the building.

I waited an hour. Four cars entered the premises, six left. No sign of Dettman or the guy who had mugged me last night. I drove down the sloped entrance and parked between a Jaguar and a Porsche.

The guy in the blue blazer eyed me suspiciously. He looked to be in his early fifties and was a couple of inches over six feet, and he had the shoulders and chest of a weight lifter, along with the stomach of a man who enjoys his beer. His face was the kind that mirrors nothing and rarely shows a change of expression, and he looked too smart to be nothing more than a glorified doorman. He had ex-cop written all over him.

"Can I help you, sir?" he asked, the voice polite, but with a bite of authority.

"I'm here to see a Ronald Dettman. He's expecting me. In the apartment of a J. Drew."

He turned to go into the glass cubicle and use the phone.

"You look familiar," I said. "I'm an ex-San Francisco cop. Were you in the department?"

He grunted. "Not here. Chicago. Retired and moved out here to get away from those winters." He looked up at the cold night sky. "Though this ain't exactly Palm Springs, is it?"

"Tell me about this J. Drew."

He pursed his lips. "This may not be much of a job,

but it's all I've got at the moment. My pension doesn't quite cut it."

I handed him one of my business cards and a twenty-dollar bill. "I just need a little background on Drew."

He palmed the twenty. "The *J* stands for Janet. She could make a living just standing still. Brunette. Gorgeous."

"She work?"

"Not that I know of."

"How about Dettman? He spend much time here?"

"Who's your client?"

"Insurance company. They're handling a big claim at Dettman's plant. He's been a pain in the ass." I pulled another twenty out of my money clip. "Cases like this the insurance company doesn't mind spending a little money."

"Dettman's here almost every day. Most nights. Her name's on the lease, but from what I hear, he's paying the rent."

"Would you know if Drew is up there now?"

"Left about an hour and a half ago."

"Dettman have any visitors in the last couple of hours?"

"A bank messenger about an hour ago. He was in and out in a few minutes."

"Thanks, Mr.——"

"You don't want to know my name, because you never talked to me," he said, going into his small office and picking up the phone. He came out in little more than a minute. "Dettman seemed surprised, but he said to send you up. The elevator is inside. On your right. Apartment 1401."

The elevator was small, but it made up for its lack of size by the quality of the carpeting and paneling. A nice watercolor of the Golden Gate Bridge adorned one wall. If it were a tad larger, and I could get a couch in, I wouldn't mind renting it, except I probably couldn't afford it.

Dettman opened the front door. He had on another one of his oversized bow ties.

"Cute, Polo. You're really cute." He opened the door just wide enough for me to enter. I kicked it in all the way and pulled out the .38 and jammed it in his stomach. "Is your strong-arm boy here, Ronnie?"

He backed away with a sneer on his face. "Nobody's here. Where are my papers?"

"I don't like paying people twice," he said, backing into a large beige-colored room decorated in oranges and browns, much like his bedroom. The walls were covered with more abstract paintings, mostly canvases of black slashes on white, à la Franz Kline. The view was magnificent. I edged over to the window and looked down on the city. I could see Green Street. My flat was no more than two blocks away. Dettman could have used a pair of binoculars or a telescope and had a ringside view of me being mugged last night.

He reached into his suit jacket and pulled out an envelope, tossing it casually in my direction. I let it bounce off me and onto the carpet.

"Where's Janet?"

"None of your fucking business. Now where are my papers?"

I used my left hand to wedge the envelope out the back of my waistband and dropped it on the floor by his feet.

"How do I know you haven't made copies?" he asked, stooping down to pick up the papers.

"How do I know you won't send someone to knock me over the head and take the money?"

His face turned ugly. "You're not worth the trouble, Polo. You're just a cheap punk, a half-assed private eye with a jail record. You're shit, Polo. Shit. Get out of here."

I kept the revolver pointed at his head and bent over to pick up the money. "Who writes your dialogue? Mr. T? Now you just cool down and remember that the next time you try cheating at cards, you may get your little fingers spanked again. And if you want to try any rough stuff, try it on someone you can handle. Like your wife."

Not bad as exit lines go, I thought, but it was wasted on Dettman. His nose was buried in the reports I'd brought back to him. The elevator seemed somehow bigger on the trip down.

8

The next morning I made a decision as to what to do with the money. Invest half of it, gamble with the other half. I took care of the gambling part with a call to a stockbroker. He had several suggestions, none of which sounded very promising. I was thinking more along the line of one of the blue chips, IBM, or some safe utilities when suddenly a thought popped into my empty head. "What about Dettman Industries?" I asked.

There was a long pause. "What do you hear about Dettman?"

"You're the broker. What do you hear?"

That long pause again. "Listen, Nick, something's going on with Dettman. There are rumors, just rumors now, that there is a possibility of a takeover. The Japanese are buying into Silicone Valley like crazy, and they're supposedly interested, but Dettman himself doesn't want to sell."

"What's the stock going for?"

"Hang on a minute." It was more like twenty seconds. "Thirteen and a quarter. Down one-eighth since yesterday."

"Okay, let's give it a try. Put an automatic sell order in at twelve dollars a share."

So now I was partners with Ron Dettman. Five hundred shares' worth. If it dropped more than a point, he'd be on his own again, but it made me feel good to think that the son of a bitch could actually make me some more money.

Now for the investment part of my scheme. I called a travel agent, made reservations for a flight to Las Vegas, and two hours later was saying Hail Marys and Our Fathers as a Boeing 727 thundered down the runway and somehow managed to lift itself off the ground.

That was Friday afternoon. On Monday morning I got back to San Francisco, lighter in everything but fond memories. I put the car in the garage and was about to go up the front stairs when a familiar voice called to me.

"Nick. I'd like to talk to you."

I squinted into the sun. The car that had pulled into my driveway was almost a duplicate of mine, except it actually *was* an unmarked police car. Inspector Bob Tehaney sat behind the wheel. He parked and got out of the car. A stockily built man in his forties with a dirty walrus mustache and wearing a blue pin-striped suit exited from the passenger's seat.

I couldn't call Tehaney a friend, but we had more than a nodding acquaintance. I had worked several different details when I was a cop, but never with Tehaney. He was in homicide.

"Hi, Bob," I said. "Come on in, I'll make some coffee."

The other man looked at the suitcase I was carrying. "Just coming back from a trip?" he asked.

Tehaney made the introductions. "Nick, this is George Melleck from the District Attorney's office."

Melleck didn't offer to shake hands. Just looked at my suitcase.

"Just got back from Vegas," I said, leading them up the stairs and into my flat.

"Make yourselves comfortable." I dropped my bag and bent down to pick up the mail inside the front door. "I'll get the coffee going."

I ground up some French roast and got good old Mr. Coffee working, all the time wondering just what the hell Tehaney wanted. And why was someone from the DA's office tagging along with him? I checked through the mail while the coffee was brewing, nothing but bills and junk, then put three steaming cups of coffee on a tray and carried them into the front room. It's my favorite room in the flat. Two walls are ceiling-to-floor used brick. There's an oversized fireplace of the same brick on the other wall. A stereo set with more gadgets than the cockpit of a 747 takes up most of the other wall. There are two good dark brown leather reclining chairs and an L-shaped sofa in off-white.

George Melleck had taken my invitation to "make yourselves comfortable" a little more seriously than I'd intended. He was bent over looking at my telephone answering machine.

"What's this all about, Bob?" I asked, passing out the coffee.

Tehaney was thin, sandy-haired, with a ruddy complexion and freckles splattered across his hands. He had more than enough time in the department to retire, but

51

he'd hang on as long as he could. He liked his work, and he was good at it. He took an appreciative sip of the coffee before answering. "Good stuff. All my wife ever gives me is that instant crap." He sighed and his tone became officious. "I'm here to ask you some questions about Allen Price."

I shrugged my shoulders. "Never heard of him."

"That's rather strange," said Melleck. "Price sent our office a glass with your fingerprints on it. Although he didn't know they were your fingerprints until we ran them through the crime lab. He thought they belonged to someone called George Walker."

I tried to look casual as I took a sip of the coffee, and studied Melleck. He had a pasty complexion and sparse hair, carefully sprayed down to cover an expanse of waxy scalp. He looked awfully ambitious for a civil servant. "Just who the hell is this Price?"

"He was an attorney," said Tehaney. "He was killed Saturday night or early Sunday morning. His body was found in his car, parked on Embarcadero, under the freeway, by the Ferry Building."

Melleck ran a stubby finger under the collar of his starched white shirt. "He was shot with a .38. According to our records, you own three handguns; a .38 revolver, a .357 Magnum revolver, and a .25 Beretta automatic."

"You know a hell of a lot more about me than I do about this Price guy. If he was an attorney, how the hell did he get the clout to run a glass with my fingerprints through the crime lab?" I turned to Tehaney. "What kind of bullshit is this? How can a civilian run my prints through the crime lab? He was a civilian, wasn't he?"

52

"Yep. Apparently he was a friend of Mr. Melleck's here."

I turned back to Melleck. "And you just let your friends use the crime lab anytime they want to? I've got a feeling my civil rights have been violated somewhere along the line."

Melleck's voice turned nasty. "I could get a warrant and turn this place over. I'm only holding back on Inspector Tehaney's advice. He seemed to think you'd be cooperative. I've got a dead man, an attorney, an officer of the court, who for some reason was interested enough in you to have your prints checked. You used a false name, George Walker, in your contact with Mr. Price; then he's found dead."

"What you've got is some buddy of yours who got hold of official police information through you. I'd say I've got a pretty good civil suit going against you, Melleck, so stick that warrant stuff up your ass."

Melleck stood up, the veins on his neck standing out. "I'll wait for you outside, Inspector," he said between clenched teeth.

He slammed the door hard enough to knock Mrs. Damonte out of her bed downstairs. Except knowing Mrs. D, she wasn't in bed. Probably standing on a ladder with her ear cocked against the ceiling.

"Excitable guy, isn't he?" said Tehaney.

"You could say that. What's his action in this?"

"Price was a friend, old college buddy apparently. Our Mr. Melleck has his eye on being the district attorney, not just an assistant. Apparently Price was pretty well connected. You're right about him running the prints through the lab. You've got him by the balls on that; still, I wouldn't put it past him to get a warrant."

"You're suggesting that I turn over my .38?"

"Any reason you shouldn't?" Tehaney asked.

"Help yourself to some more coffee. I'll be right back."

I went down the back stairs to the basement. My stomach settled down when I felt the butt of the revolver safely tucked away in the car's headrest. I pocketed it and carried it back to my flat. Mrs. D pursed her lips and shook her head at me as I passed her back window.

Tehaney was lighting a cigarette, scorching it halfway down with a throwaway lighter. He still smoked Lucky unfilters for some reason.

I flipped open the gun's cylinder and pushed the bullets out. "Here it is, Bob. You want the shells?"

"Maybe one wouldn't hurt." He put the smoke down long enough to pick up the gun and one bullet. I thought for sure he was going to sniff the barrel, but he just dropped it in his suit pocket. "What can you tell me about this guy Price, Nick?"

"Not much. I don't even know if we're talking about the same guy. I did get into a card game with an attorney named Al. I never paid any attention to his last name."

"Price was fifty-one years of age. White, maybe a little Oriental blood in there somewhere. Just under six feet tall. Had an office on Montgomery Street. Married. Lived in Belvedere, so he must have been successful. No kids. Shot twice, both in the head, while sitting in the driver's seat of his Jaguar. The car's window was down. That's about all I know about him right now."

"And I'm your only suspect?"

54

"You're Melleck's only suspect. I wouldn't get too cute with him, Nick. He's no dummy."

Tehaney chain-lit another Lucky while I went back for the coffeepot.

"Did this Price ever get the information about my prints?"

"Saturday morning."

"What if I call you tomorrow, Bob? You'll probably have the lab tests back on my gun by then, and maybe I'll be able to find out something on Price myself in the meantime."

He drew deeply on his cigarette and puffed the smoke toward the ceiling. "Like maybe just where and when you were in this card game with him, and who the other players were?"

"Stuff like that, yeah."

"Anybody in Vegas that will remember where you were late Saturday or early Sunday morning?"

"I'm not even sure where I was myself. I bounced from casino to casino, spreading the money around."

Tehaney sighed and got to his feet. "I know what you mean. I do the same thing. But I only play bingo."

9

After Tehaney left I splashed some Amaretto in the remains of my coffee and tried to figure out just why the hell the late Al Price had gone through the trouble of checking on my fingerprints. I remembered sitting with him and the English guy, Charlie something-or-other, and having a drink after the poker game. What the hell was Price going to do when he found out who I was?

I went back to the front room and checked my telephone answering machine. No wonder George Melleck had been hovering over it earlier. The little bright green digital call counter was showing that forty-seven calls had come in. Forty-seven! I don't get that many calls some months.

I rewound the tape and played them back. The first one was from my broker confirming the purchase order of Dettman Industry stock. There were seven calls with no messages. Then a voice I remembered, and it made the hairs on my back stand up like the bristles of a porcupine in heat.

"Mr. Polo, or should I say Walker. This is Al Price. We met at the Sequioa Club the other night. I'd very much like to talk to you. It is now Saturday and, let's see, a little after noon. If you'd be good enough to call me at 876-9605, I would appreciate it."

I stopped the machine, wound it back and listened again, for what, I don't know. Saturday at noon. Some twelve hours later, the poor guy was dead.

I started the tape again. More calls with no messages. Dozens of the damn things. A call from a friend asking if I wanted to go to the ball game next weekend. More blank calls, and finally one from Inspector Bob Tehaney, saying it was Monday morning and that he wanted to see me.

That was it. Out of forty-seven calls, there were four messages. I was trying to figure out who my bashful caller was when the phone rang and startled the hell out of me.

"Hello," I said. Simple but effective.

"Oh, Mr. Polo, I'm so glad you're in. I've been trying to get you all weekend. This is Alicia Dettman. I want to see you as soon as possible."

She was speaking in a rush, all her words running together. "Take it easy, Mrs. Dettman. What's this all about?"

"Well, it's not anything I'd like to talk about on the phone. But I really have to meet you."

"I'm not so sure your husband would be happy to see us get together."

"Are you frightened of Ronald?"

"No. But from the look of your eye the other night, maybe you should be. How did you get my name?"

She laughed. "Your name has been quite popular around here the last few days. There were usually a few

57

descriptive adjectives in front of it. Whatever you did to Ron, you really got him mad."

"And what is it I can do for you?"

"Meet me, and I'll tell you everything. Please?"

"Okay. Where and when?"

"What about your office? As soon as possible."

"Let's make it around noon. I'll have lunch ready." I gave her the address. "Park right in the driveway; there's never any parking available. If a little lady in a black dress gives you any trouble, just tell her you're visiting me."

I called Randall at the bank but he was "in a meeting." I showered, shaved, and changed into slacks and a dark blue sport shirt from Polo's. (How many guys get to have their names on the labels of their shirts? Sure, Mr. Arrow and Mr. Van Heusen, but how many others?) I put on a chef's apron, then went about the serious business of putting together a serious lunch. After three days of Vegas food, my stomach was screaming for something that actually tasted real and unfrozen. I took a large bowl from the kitchen cabinet and went out and down to the backyard. Mrs. D's garden. Now I know that world hunger is a very real and terrible problem, and I don't want to make light of it, but if you sent Mrs. D anywhere in the world with one zucchini plant, I guarantee you that in just a few weeks the whole place would be covered with zucchini. She had the yard neatly laid out. Chard, green onions, Italian beans against one fence. The tomatoes in the center, where they got the most sun. Artichokes and three kinds of lettuce against the back fence, and peppers, sweet basil, and the ever-present zucchini against the other fence. There were tubs of herbs—rosemary, tarragon, mint, parsley, and oregano—spread around the yard.

58

It wasn't just the fact that Mrs. D liked gardening; she provided one of North Beach's best restaurants with a daily supply of the stuff.

I started with the zucchini, making sure to get the ones with the great big white-and-yellow flower that blossoms on the end, several handfuls of the beans, a half dozen ripe tomatoes, lots of the basil, and some parsley, oregano, and rosemary.

I stopped at the cage housing Bambi and Boom-Boom, Mrs. D's two hen chickens. There were a couple of old Safeway cartons full of eggs neatly stacked alongside the cage. I picked the one from the bottom, knowing that Mrs. D always kept the freshest ones there. Mrs. D peered out her window at me. I smiled, showing her my treasure, and she gave me a sour nod, seeing that there'd be less to sell to the restaurant now.

Everything but the eggs went into a colander for a rinse, and then the vegetables went into a pot to be parboiled. I threw chunks of Parmesan cheese into the food processor and cut up the beans and zucchini, mixed them with eggs, garlic, and some of the cheese, some oregano and rosemary, and shoved the mixture into the oven.

The basil went into a blender with more garlic, more cheese, and some butter and olive oil and just a sprinkle of pine nuts.

The zucchini flowers were dipped in egg yolk and bread crumbs, then fried in olive oil.

I started the water to boil for the pasta and was just opening a bottle of Soave Classico when the doorbell rang.

Alicia Dettman was all in black, but unlike Mrs. Damonte, she wasn't going to a funeral. Not in that outfit. The pants were leather, and tight. The top had a big industrial-sized zipper that went from chin to tummy. Right now it was at about half-mast. A black hairband held back the blond locks. Sunglasses with frames as big as coffee saucers covered her eyes.

She dropped the glasses down her nose and peered at me over the rims. "You didn't have to get all dressed up just for me," she said.

I could see the edge of a shiner behind the glasses. "Come on in. Lunch will be ready in a few minutes."

She followed me to the kitchen, stopping to peek into doorways as we walked down the hall.

"This is quite a place. Is there a Mrs. Polo?"

"Not anymore. Care for a glass of wine?"

"Sure."

I poured us both a glass of Soave. "Sit down and relax. I've got to get back to the stove."

She sat down on the edge of a kitchen chair for a minute, then was up, looking out the window, peering into the open cabinets, checking the contents of the sink.

"You really seem to like cooking, don't you?"

"I like eating," I said, dropping the pasta into the boiling water. The zucchini flowers needed turning.

"What are those?"

I told her.

"And you really eat them?"

"They're delicious." Her glass was empty already. "Have some more wine."

She refilled her glass, then went over and peeked into the refrigerator. "Amazing. Ron wouldn't know how to make toast."

"Not much money in making toast. He seems to do all right at what he's good at."

60

"What he's good at is being a prick."

I couldn't argue with that. "What did you want to talk to me about, Alicia?"

"First, I wanted to thank you for taking care of me the other night. I woke up all nicely tucked in. That was you, wasn't it?"

"You looked comfortable enough on the couch. I didn't want to wake you."

"You couldn't have woken me with a bullhorn. I was out of it." She stared down into her wineglass, then, with a flick of the wrist, tossed down what was left in the glass. "I drink too much. Especially when I'm nervous, Mr. Polo."

"Call me Nick. And if I'm making you nervous, have some more of the wine."

She sighed, inhaling heavily, doing wonderful things to the front of her zippered top. "I don't know exactly what you did to Ron, but whatever it was, I've never seen him madder. He kept talking about killing you. He was throwing things at the wall. Kicking the furniture. It was wonderful."

"Whatever turns you on," I said, going to the oven and taking out the frittata. "You can make yourself useful by setting the table."

The noodles were done, nice and al dente. I drained them, put them back in the pot and mixed in the pesto sauce. I sliced the tomatoes, covered them with a light coating of the grated cheese and parsley, and put everything on the table.

She picked at everything as if it were going to explode at first, then began to eat, fast and without finesse. The zucchini flowers got raves. We had gone through the bottle of wine by now and she asked if she might have more.

"Do you have any champagne?"

"Sure."

A bottle of Domaine Chandon Blanc de Noirs joined the table, along with fresh glasses.

"That was fantastic," she said, her plate scraped clean. "I don't remember when I've eaten that much." She burped lightly, then laughed. "You did use a lot of garlic, didn't you?"

"My mother put garlic in everything but the coffee."

She frowned, watching a thin line of bubbles rise up through the pale copper-colored wine. "Would you kill my husband for me, Mr. Polo?"

"No."

Her lips twisted wryly. "That's it? Just a simple No? No explanations: no 'You shouldn't talk like that'? No 'You can't go around asking people to kill your husband'?"

"Have you been asking many people?"

"You're the first. But maybe not the last." She took off the sunglasses. A dark blue bruise just about circled her whole left eye. "He beats me, Mr. Polo. Quite often. Usually he makes sure the bruises don't show. He's quite clever about just how and where he beats me."

"Divorce him."

"I'm afraid he wants to divorce me."

"Let him."

Her lower lip curled. "Don't give me dumb, simple answers. If it was all that easy, I'd have divorced him years ago."

"What's making it so difficult? The divorce rules are pretty simple in this state. You'd end up with about half of what he's worth. Which should keep you in all the tight leather pants you'll ever need for the rest of your life."

"Ronald is a bastard. A real bastard. If I divorce him, I won't get a fucking cent."

She reached over for the champagne bottle and topped off our glasses. "He's got evidence that I've been seeing other people. Some of these people may not be what society would think of as very nice people. He'd spread the evidence around. To everyone."

"So you want to find someone to kill your husband, then you'll inherit everything and live happily ever after."

"His will is quite complicated. Even if I do inherit, most of the money is tied up in trusts. I wouldn't starve, but . . ." She put her sunglasses back on. "I want to neutralize him. Get something on Ron that's as bad as what he's got on me. Something I can use before he just forces me into a divorce where I come out with nothing. I don't want to sound like a money-grabbing wife, but I've put up with the bastard for eleven years now. I deserve something."

"Why did you put up with him that long?"

She ran a finger around the rim of the wineglass. "The first seven years were heaven. Then hell entered the picture."

"Just what kind of evidence are we talking about?"

"Pictures. Dirty pictures, I guess you could say. Tape recordings. He played a few for me." She tried smiling but it didn't come off. "I didn't realize I was so vocal."

"What do you know about your husband's relationship with Al Price?"

The question snapped her out of her self-guilt. "Al?

He was Ron's attorney. Or one of them, anyway. He died. It was in the papers."

I got up and started taking the plates to the sink. "I'll make a deal with you, Alicia. You find out what you can about your husband's dealings with Al Price, and I'll see what I can do about getting something on Ron, something you can use to bargain with him." I held out a hand. "Deal?"

She took my hand in both of hers and pulled me close to her. "Deal," she said, her voice turning husky. The ring on the zipper nestled between her breasts was just the right size for a man's finger to fit in. The wine and the lack of sleep were an excuse I could have used. The fact that Alicia was a beautiful, available woman in need of a strong shoulder to cry on was another excuse. Neither excuse would have cut the mustard with the sainted nun, Sister Mary Holy Card, who had taught me the right and wrongs of life from kindergarten to the eighth grade. The truth was I had been dying to stick my finger in that ring from the moment Alicia came in the front door. I was right. It was a perfect fit.

10

Pillow talk. An old-fashioned term. I got some very new-fashioned information from Alicia, most of it about the way her husband had been treating her. She also supplied me with some simple background information on Al Price; his home address in Belvedere, his wife's name, Maya, whom she called the Dragon Lady, and the fact that Al had made several passes at her. All uncompleted, according to Alicia. She also gave me her husband's birth date and said she would call me later with his social security number.

I had no idea just how much of what Alicia told me was the truth, but one thing she wasn't lying about: She was very vocal. If Mrs. Damonte had understood a little more English, her ears would have been burning. I hoped she wouldn't ask me for a translation.

After Alicia left I called Paul Randall's office again. His secretary said he was still "unavailable."

"Please tell him that Nick Polo called, and that I'm

going to meet with the police tomorrow morning regarding the murder of our card-playing friend." I severed the connection before his secretary had a chance to reply.

Randall called back three minutes later.

"What the hell do you think you're doing, leaving a message like that with my secretary?" he demanded in a hoarse, reedy voice.

"I left a nice polite message earlier and didn't hear from you."

"What's this about you meeting with the police department?"

"Al Price didn't trust me very much. He swiped a glass from the Sequoia Club. With my prints on it. He had a friend in the DA's office run the prints and came up with my name. The police are naturally curious."

"Shit!" was his only comment. Then, "We better meet on this. Can you come down here right now? No, wait, not at the office. Can you meet me at . . . oh, the St. Francis Hotel, the Rose Compass bar, in, say, an hour?"

"I'll see you there."

Randall was waiting for me when I got there. The Rose Compass is located in a spot right off the hotel's main lobby. A handsome young man who looks as if he just stepped out of one of those perfume ads greets you warmly and lets you follow his seven-hundred-dollar suit across the beautiful Persian carpeting to a small round table. Randall was sitting alone, a drink in front of him. A tall young cocktail waitress in a red silk pantsuit asked me what I wanted before I was even seated.

"Club soda, please," I said.

The bar itself was jammed with mostly single men,

dressed in much the same expensive manner as the man who had lead me to the table. The tables themselves were filled with bored businessmen and couples having a drink before dinner and the show. Someone who knew what he was doing was playing Gershwin on a grand piano.

"I don't like this police business, Polo. I don't like it at all." He shook his head slowly, then pointed his chin at me. "I never should have hired you. It was a mistake, damn it. A big mistake."

"Thanks for showing all that confidence in me. If I knew you were going to be so helpful, I would have just dumped my guts to the police this morning."

"You've already spoken to them?"

"Yep." We waited while my club soda was being delivered. Nice tall glass filled with ice. Small dish of lemon and lime wedges. The soda still in its frosted bottle. Classy. And why not? They charged eight-fifty for the damn thing.

"What did you tell the police?" Randall asked anxiously after the waitress had left.

"Not much. Just that I never even knew Price's last name until they mentioned it to me."

"They?"

"A police inspector named Bob Tehaney, and an assistant district attorney, George Melleck. They both came to my place this morning."

"God," Randall groaned. "The district attorney's office too."

"What did you expect, the Boy Scouts? Price was murdered. Now you are, or were, a client, so I have certain loyalties to you, but they stop when there's been a murder. Tomorrow morning I'm going to meet with Inspector Tehaney and tell him just how and where I met Al Price."

Randall made interlocking rings on the tabletop with the wet bottom of his glass. "You have to talk with them, but just how much do you have to tell them? Surely Al's death had nothing to do with our card game."

"Why was he so interested in me?"

Randall shrugged. "He must have known that you cheated on that last hand. Maybe he was just curious, I don't know."

"Did he call you after the game?"

"No." The answer came quick. Maybe too quick.

"Did your bank do much business with Price?"

He spread his hands. "We do business with a lot of attorneys. I can't—"

"Bullshit," I said louder than necessary. An elderly woman with snow-white hair sitting across from us gave me a disgusted look.

"Randall, stop playing at being a banker. We're talking murder."

"Al Price was involved in a lot of real estate transactions. That was his specialty. He represented various individuals, corporations from overseas. He put the deals together, and we supplied the financing on many of them."

"Overseas money. Japanese?"

"Certainly. They've been very active in the markets here in the Bay area."

"What about their interest in taking over Dettman Industries? Was Price involved in that?"

"Where did you get that information?" Randall asked, the pious banker once again.

"You can't keep something like that quiet. Was he?"

"I think so."

"What's your opinion of Alicia Dettman?"

Randall's eyebrows cocked into a questioning arc. "Why, she's a wonderful, sweet woman. Why do you ask? What's that got to do with all of this?"

"I've heard that she and Ron aren't exactly lovebirds anymore."

Randall leaned across the table, his voice lowered. "I think you'd be better off if you just stuck to your own problems, Mr. Polo."

"One of my problems is that right now I'm apparently the prime suspect in a murder case. I'm going to have to have a list of all the men in that card game."

"What for?"

"To give to the police. Or would you rather have them get the list from you? Where were you the night Price was shot, anyway?"

Randall stood up abruptly and for a moment I thought he was either going to stomp out or stomp on me. Then he sat down and took a leather pocket secretary from his suit pocket. He used a gold Cross pen and neatly printed out a list of names.

"I suppose this means that the police will be talking to everyone who was at the card game, including me."

"I wouldn't be surprised."

"This is very embarrassing for me."

"Think how I feel."

He looked up briefly, his gray eyes frosty. "You've been a disappointment, Mr. Polo. A bitter disappointment."

He left the list on the table, then got up and walked away. I was studying the list when the waitress returned and handed me the bill. Nineteen dollars and forty-seven cents. No wonder Randall left in a hurry.

11

The morning *Chronicle* was one of those good-news, bad-news deals. The good news was that Dettman Industries went up a full dollar a share. The bad news was a story on page 2:

PRIVATE EYE QUESTIONED IN LAWYER'S
MURDER

Police have interviewed private investigator Nick Polo regarding the murder of attorney Allen Price, who was shot to death late last Saturday night. According to sources in the department, Polo, an ex-San Francisco policeman who once served time in federal prison for receiving stolen property, was questioned regarding his prior contacts with Price.

Price was considered an expert in real-estate and business mergers. Price was found in his car, a dark green Jaguar, parked under the Embarcadero Freeway.

Police sources stated that they have found no motive for the crime. Price was wearing a valuable

70

watch and his wallet was still on his person when the body was found.

Not much of an article. It was accompanied by an unflattering picture of me. Of course, not too many mug shots are flattering. I liked the part about the stolen property. Actually, I never thought it was stolen. Just found. Like a half-million dollars. An attorney had hired me to find his client. And I did. Dead of a drug overdose in a run-down motel room. He was from somewhere in Latin America, with no known relatives. And he had this suitcase bulging with cash. The attorney and I argued for maybe a good two minutes on whether or not to turn the money over to the cops. We both agreed it would just cause a lot of unnecessary bookkeeping, so we split the money. And everyone lived happily ever after, for about a week. Then the attorney got nervous and decided that he should turn his part of the loot in. And turn me in too. He got a friendly handshake, a pat on the back, and I got seven months in a federal crossbar hotel.

Have you heard the one about the pope, a bishop, and an attorney all dying on the same day? They go right up to the Pearly Gates and Saint Peter welcomes them with open arms. He takes them on a tour of Paradise. First he stops at a nice little one-bedroom place, with a neat kitchen, a color TV, and tells the bishop that it's all his.

The next stop is a two-bedroom place, bigger kitchen, bigger TV, and he tells the pope that this is his place.

Then he takes the attorney to this huge mansion—big swimming pool, private golf course, angels built like

71

Lonnie Anderson flying all over the place—and he tells the attorney all this is his.

The attorney can't understand it. "Saint Peter," he says, "but you gave that bishop just a small apartment. And the pope, his place wasn't much better. Why am I getting all of this?

"Well," Saint Peter says, "we have dozens of popes up here, and thousands of bishops, but you're the first attorney we've ever had."

I parked under a sign that said "Police Vehicles Only" in an alleyway alongside the Hall of Justice. Bob Tehaney was waiting for me in his office. He took me into a six-by-six square interrogation room. It had a wooden table bolted to a wall, the top crisscrossed with cigarette burns, and two hard-backed wooden chairs, one on either side of the table. "Spartan" would be a charitable description.

"First off, Nick, I want you to know I had nothing to do with that article in this morning's paper."

"I never thought you did, Bob," I said, gingerly sliding into one of the chairs."

The door opened and George Melleck came in, dragging a chair behind him. He had a self-satisfying grin on his face. He fingered loose his tie as he sat down.

Tehaney dropped a brick-red manila file folder on the table and lit up a Lucky. "The lab completed the tests on your gun, Nick. No match-up. Remind me to give it to you when we're finished."

I went through the whole story, leaving out some minor details, such as just how much money was bet at the poker game, the attack on me in front of my flat, and, of course, my borrowing those papers from Dettman's desk.

Melleck was fidgeting in his chair, like a kid in a church pew waiting to get to a baseball game. Names like Paul Randall and Ronald Dettman were big league, and I could almost see the little wheels in his brain spinning, trying to figure out just how to handle them.

When I was through with my spiel, Melleck stood up, stretched, then said a line I'd heard a hundred times on TV and in the movies, but never actually thought I'd hear in real life.

"Okay, Polo. That's enough for now. But stick around. I want you available."

Tehaney pointed a finger like a truncheon at him. "I'm in charge of this investigation, Melleck, and if you leak one more phony story to the papers, you're going to find yourself off this case."

Melleck sneered down at him. "Who the hell do you think you're talking to!"

"To a man who let a civilian have use of the police department crime lab. I've already spoken to the chief about that this morning. He's kind of touchy about those things, you know."

Melleck turned on his heels and slammed the door behind him. I'd only seen the guy twice, and both times he slammed the door. Maybe that's the way he always leaves a room.

Tehaney left without saying anything. The file folder was lying there on the table. Very tempting. But I waited.

Tehaney came back in a few minutes carrying two cups of coffee in Styrofoam cups.

"Nothing like that stuff you serve up, but it'll have to do," he said, handing me one of the cups.

"I've got to go over to the lab, pick up your gun. It'll

take me about ten minutes, Nick." His watery-blue eyes went from me to the folder.

When he left I took a sip of the coffee, somehow managed to get it down without gagging, then went to work on the file.

There were several pictures of Price slumped over the wheel of his car. Grisly close-ups of the entry wounds. Right in the face. He must have been looking up at his killer when the bullets were fired.

The body inventory showed a Rolex watch, gold cuff links, a wallet filled with the usual ID, driver's license, business cards; plenty of plastic money, a MasterCard, a Visa, several gas credit cards, and a thousand-dollar bill. And a gold money clip in the shape of a dollar sign stuffed with four hundred and forty-six dollars.

The only other thing of interest were two bottles of Dom Perignon in a paper bag in the car's trunk.

I copied down Price's date of birth, social security number, home and business addresses, and phone numbers.

The report of the officers who found the body showed that they had been on routine patrol and noticed the Jaguar. It looked out of place. No witnesses were around the scene, and, according to the rest of the reports in the file, none had come forward to date.

There was a hand-scribbled notation on the district attorney's letterhead to Tehaney from George Melleck. Stapled to it was a brief report from the crime lab showing that the prints on the glass supplied by Melleck belonged to Nicholas Polo.

I put the file back together neatly and had it centered on the table when Tehaney came back.

"More coffee?" he asked, handing me my .38 revolver.

"No, thanks. What's next on the Price case?"

He got another cigarette going before answering. "I'll have to speak to a few of those people from the card game. Probably start with this Randall first. Unless Melleck is already sitting on his lap. What kind of a guy is he?"

"A banker. Smart, cold, tough. He's not going to be overly happy about seeing you."

"Most people aren't," Tehaney said with a grin.

The robbery detail was right down the hall from Homicide. Luckily Paul Paulsen, a big, easygoing Swede, still worked robbery. We had gone through the police academy together and remained good friends. I gave him a song and dance about a client who was being threatened.

"I got a look at the guy, Paul. He looked familiar. I'd like to run through your mug shots."

"Be my guest." He lead me back to the room where they kept the huge canvas-bound mug-shot books.

"Take your time," Paul said, never once mentioning the article in the morning's paper. You can always tell your real friends by what they don't say.

I leafed through the mug shots. Whoever reshot the *Untouchables* missed a real bet by not checking these guys out first. I mean, we are talking major ugly here. There were some familiar faces; guys I had arrested, a couple of guys I went to high school with and never knew they'd been busted, and finally my friend with the pocked nose and yellow teeth. I copied down the name and number under the photograph: "Ray Denko, S.F. #64281," and gave the information to Paul Paulsen. He punched the data into a computer, and moments later the printer clattered to life and out popped Denko's rap sheet. It showed his social security number, driver's license number, and an address that was four years old. Ray had left a few footprints in the sands of crime: several armed-robbery arrests, no convictions; two burglaries, one conviction; a few petty thefts, drunk driving, and one rape. The only listed conviction was on the one burglary. So Ray was either smart, lucky, or connected.

I pocketed the rap sheet, thanked Paulsen, and headed for home.

12

The first thing I did when I got back to the flat was make some decent coffee. While that was brewing I checked my answering machine. A brief message in a soft, sexy little girl's voice, a statutory-rape voice. Alicia Dettman leaving me her husband's social security number.

I poured a nice cup of the coffee and made the long commute to my office, which is right across the hallway from my bedroom. The room is ten by twelve, has three black metal filing cabinets, a black metal desk, the top littered with a Rolodex, staplers, a stack of manila file folders, an adding machine, and an electric typewriter. There are two chairs, one the standard swivel-back type, the other backless, with a place to rest your knees on. In the corner is a small copy machine, and against the wall with a window overlooking Mrs. D's garden sits the one indispensable item in the modern private investigator's inventory.

Sure, I know in the good old days all a guy needed

was a good hat, a trench coat, a shoulder-holstered .45 automatic, and a half-filled bottle of Old Grand Dad in the bottom drawer of his desk. Those days are gone, I'm sorry to say, folks. What you got to have now is a computer.

I sat down in that funny little chair with the knee rests and turned on the almighty IBM, wondering if, somewhere deep inside its soul, there were some parts manufactured by Dettman Industries. It whirled and gurgled to life. I slipped in a floppy disk labeled SMARTCOM, and the machine digested it quickly, then punched a few programmed buttons. Within seconds I was hooked up to a data base in Los Angeles.

I entered the names, birthdays, and social security numbers of Ronald Dettman, Allen Price, and Ray Denko. The amber-and-black screen asked me a few questions, which I dutifully answered, telling it, or them, or whoever was on the other side of the screen, that I wanted driver's license records, credit reports, and lists of all the civil suits these fine and worthy gentleman were involved in.

The machine hummed a final greeting and the screen advised me that the session had now come to an end.

I freshened the coffee and was debating on just what to do for the next few hours while I waited for the computer to report back to me, when the phone rang.

"Mr. Polo, this is Maya Price. I wonder if you might be available this afternoon."

"Yes, I'm available, Mrs. Price. What did you have in mind? Have you spoken to the police?"

"Oh, many times. Rest assured I do not think you are in any way responsible for my husband's death. I want

78

to see you on a business matter. I think it could be most profitable for you." Her voice was flat, as if she was reciting something from a book.

She gave me her address and I told her I'd be there within the hour. I decided to take the .38, and a mini voice-activated tape recorder.

It was a bright, sunny afternoon, not a cloud in the sky. I drove out to the Marina and up Doyle Drive to the bridge of bridges, the Golden Gate, famous in song, photographed millions of times, everybody's favorite bridge, except for those who have to drive across it daily. There are only six lanes, and they poke these funny little yellow cones in holes in the road so that they can alter the number of lanes to help the congested rush-hour traffic. That means that there are only two lanes of traffic going either north, or south, each day. And only those in a hurry, or too stupid to know better, would ever travel in the outside lane, because the only thing that separates you from the oncoming traffic is the above-mentioned little plastic cones. There's a major head-on collision every few months. People die terribly in their mangled cars, the papers run headlines, print the grisly statistics of prior accidents; committees are formed to study the problem, suggestions are made. Then nothing is done and everything returns to status quo until the next big accident, when the whole merry-go-round starts up again.

I hugged the curb lane, sneaking occasional glances at the bay. Sailboats, looking like neatly folded handkerchiefs against the blue water, scooted in front of the big tankers steaming in and out of harbor. The tourists were loving it, hanging over the guardrails, cameras at the ready.

Belvedere is a tiny little island shaped roughly like a shark's head, snuggled right next to Tiburon, which, appropriately enough, means "shark" in Spanish. The average home in Belvedere goes for seven hundred thousand dollars, and those are the handyman specials.

The Price place was on Beach Road, on the sheltered side of the island, on top of a hill, looking down on Belvedere Cove and the Corinthian Yacht Club. A cultivated wilderness of trees, shrubs, and rocks cascaded down to the bay. The house was a multi-level affair painted a light green that blended into the hillside's oak and pine trees. I parked underneath a huge oak tree, activated the mini recorder, which was safely snuggled in my inside coat pocket, then followed a path of concrete steps set in crushed rock over a small bridge that crossed a pond filled with lilies and hundreds of white, silver, and gold carp, some big enough for mounting, to the front door. A red bougainvillea brushed against the wall in the afternoon breeze as I rang the bell.

Beige silk curtains drew back on the window next to the door. A tiny woman was standing there. She couldn't have been more than five feet tall, with jet-black hair, the bangs cut straight across her forehead. She was wearing a bright green pantsuit and had a white scarf tied around her throat.

She questioned me with her eyes.

"I'm Nick Polo," I said. "Mrs. Price?"

She nodded briefly and the curtains closed.

13

She looked even smaller up close. She held the door open and I took the tiny offered hand. "My condolences on the death of your husband," I said as I entered the house.

She had high cheekbones, absolutely flawless-looking skin the color of light teak. Her eyes were large, doelike, her hair so black it had hints of blue in it. She was Eurasian, but it was impossible to guess just what the mixture was. She was literally one of those few women so lovely they took your breath away.

She was also a mind reader. "My father was French, my mother Hawaiian," she said, smiling at the embarrassed look on my face.

"Excuse me for staring."

She fluttered a hand. "Sooner or later everyone seems to want to know my background. It's something of an obsession with you Mainlanders. Can I fix you something to drink?"

I followed her into a large living room. The floor was

quartzite. A black baby grand piano matched the lacquered tables. The couch and chairs were upholstered in chenille in a color that matched the rough plaster walls. Two bronze deer, half life-sized, stood in front of a window that took up most of the far wall.

"No, nothing for me, Mrs. Price."

She apologized for the mess, which consisted of a few magazines out of place on the coffee table. "I want to hire you, Mr. Polo, to find something that was taken from my husband the night he was killed."

"The police report doesn't show that anything was missing."

She sank gracefully into one of the chenille chairs. "Ah, you have read the report?"

"I got a quick glance at it while the police were questioning me."

"They do not know anything was missing. And I would just as soon they never find out."

"Just what was it, Mrs. Price?"

She fluttered those little hands again. "Please, call me Maya. What is missing is something that you once had in your possession, I believe, Mr. Polo. Documents relating to research in neurocomputing. Do you recall seeing those documents?"

"I've never even heard of neurocomputing."

"But you did see the documents, didn't you? You took them from Ronald Dettman's desk. And you sold them to him for fourteen thousand dollars."

"Wrong."

"Wrong? Please, Mr. Polo, don't insult me. My husband was Ronald Dettman's attorney. He told him everything."

"Believe it or not, Maya, sometimes people don't tell their attorneys the truth."

She perched on the edge of her chair with catlike trimness, one hand over each knee. "You deny that you took the documents? You deny that you sold them back to Ronald Dettman?

"If this was a court of law, I might deny it. Let's just say that right now I mean that what you're saying is wrong."

The hands didn't flutter this time. They chopped the air like karate blows. "It is foolish for you to tell such lies. I know you had the documents, and you are not a fool, so you made copies of them. I want those documents. I will pay you a very handsome sum. Say twenty-five thousand dollars. For either the copies, or the originals that were taken from my husband."

"Are you sure your husband had them at the time of his murder?"

"Positive."

"Let's say that I once did have these documents. And that I returned them to Dettman. How did your husband get ahold of them?"

"That is of no concern to you. You are in a position to make a substantial sum of money. I suggest you take it."

"If I had made copies, and unfortunately I didn't, I wonder what Ronald Dettman would pay for them?"

She uncoiled herself from the chair and stood rigidly, as if she was about to refuse a blindfold. "I would not advise you to make a game of this. Do you or do you not have the copies?"

"No. But if I can locate the ones taken from your

husband, I'd be more than happy to hand them over to you."

Her face hardened. "Good-bye, Mr. Polo," she said, swiveled on a heel and walked briskly out of the room.

As they say in the movies, I let myself out.

Traffic was heavy going north across the bridge. The cones had magically separated traffic lanes again, so there were only two lanes southbound into the city. I dutifully hugged the curb lane, my mind on Maya Price. Hardly the grieving widow. What had Alicia called her? The Dragon Lady. She came close to having smoke and fire pouring out of her nostrils at the end there. A big camper was dawdling along at about twenty miles an hour in front of me, so I pulled over into the second lane. My mind was still on Maya Price when I felt the nudge. A heavy dark car had pulled in front of the camper and was bumping me into the oncoming traffic. I jammed my foot on the brake and pushed hard on the horn as I skidded into the mass of oncoming traffic. The tip of my bumper was caught and I suddenly spun out, luckily to my right, bouncing heavily against the front of that big camper. There was a sickening crunching sound as the Ford's right side collided with the left side of the camper. It dragged me a few yards ahead, then I broke free, almost spinning out of control again.

I figure I added about forty-five minutes to the commute time for the poor souls leaving San Francisco for Marin. Even though the accident didn't block their lanes, the rubberneckers all had to slow down for a look.

The guy driving the camper turned out to be a good chap. He was with his wife and three kids, visiting from Wood River, Illinois, which I learned, only because he told me four times, was just north of St. Louis.

84

He had a kitchen in the camper and he poured me a cup of coffee, lacing it with Wild Turkey, as we waited for the tow-truck operator.

His camper had hardly suffered any damage at all. But the Ford, hardly a winner before, looked like hell now.

I rode with the tow-truck operator to a garage off Lombard, took what little of value there was from the car, including the .38 and a spare camera from the trunk, and grabbed a cab home.

I reported the accident to the friendly recorded voice that answered the phone for my insurance company. Why is it that the recorded messages usually sound pleasant, but when you talk to the people in person they're so damn grouchy?

I went through the prescribed motions with the computer again. The information was ready and soon the printer was clattering away at high speed. Twelve pages' worth of high speed.

Ronald Dettman's name was shown alongside Dettman Industries as being involved in twenty-six separate civil actions in San Francisco County alone. The plaintiffs were usually company or corporate names. There was one suit for divorce, filed by Alicia, two years back. So she had tried it once, and failed.

Allen Price had his share of suits too, and in several he was a co-defendant with Dettman. Rotten apple, rotten tree, I guess.

There was nothing startling on their driver's licenses: Dettman's showed the right home address, rather than his hideaway on Taylor Street. Price's showed his office address, not the Belvedere house.

Raymond Denko was clear of civil suits. No doubt he was too busy with the criminal stuff to get involved in some petty civil problem.

His driver's license was good, though. It listed an address on 479 Hyde Street in San Francisco.

I put the mini recorder with the tape still inside it in the office desk, then, since whoever was out to get me seemed damn serious about it, I decided it was time to carry some serious armament. I keep the .357 Magnum in a bureau drawer in my bedroom. It's a big gun. Too big, but it certainly seemed the right size now. I got the shoulder holster, which is made out of about the same amount of leather they use on a thoroughbred's saddle, adjusted it so it was somewhat less than painful, added the reasonably sized but underpowered .25 Beretta with its ankle holster, and dropped my handy-dandy Swiss Army knife into my jacket pocket, then walked down two blocks to the 626 Green Street Restaurant and had a nice solitary meal. I tried to make some sense of just what the hell was going on as I worked my way through minestrone, salad, and osso buco.

I'd never even gotten a glimpse of the driver of the car that pushed me into traffic roulette. It was possible for someone to follow me all the way over to Belvedere without my noticing it. If you're not looking for a tail, you'll never see one. From now on, I'd be looking for one. Would Dettman be having me followed? More than likely, it was Maya Price. But why take a chance on having me killed just after leaving her place? Maybe the chance was just too good an opportunity for the killer, or, as I should gratefully say, attempted killer, to turn down.

And how did Maya know so much about my dealings

with Dettman? Would Dettman really tell his attorney that much? He seemed like a man who'd keep all the deep dark secrets to himself.

I had an espresso and a Calvados for dessert and had the waiter call me a cab.

Number 479 Hyde Street was an old battered graystone corner building at the fringes of the Tenderloin District. The Tenderloin had gone through a lot of changes over the years. At one time it had been the spot for after-hour jazz joints and downstairs gambling rooms. Then the pimps and the whores had taken over the streets, followed quickly by the drug dealers. Frail senior citizens, their shoulders bent in surrender, walked nervously down the streets, their eyes shooting back and forth like ping-pong balls, hurrying to get to their cold, one-room apartments, just to survive for one more day. But now the streets and apartments were filling with bright-eyed Asian kids, living five or six to a room with their parents, throwing balls and tossing Frisbees past the glazed eyes of the unisex whores and drugged-out losers huddled in the doorways of the boarded-up shops and hotels.

A scratched and faded old brass plaque with the name "Capella Apartments" barely visible hung over the mailbox nameplates at 479 Hyde, attesting to what must have been better times.

Denko's name wasn't listed on the mailbox, but then nearly half of the apartments had a blank spot next to their numbers.

I pushed the button for unit 101. An old man with skin as fine and transparent as parchment opened the front door. He was wearing suspenders over a pair of old tweed pants. If the suspenders hadn't been there, the pants would have dropped to his ankles.

"You the manager?" I asked.

"Yup."

I debated on whether to show him my old inspector's badge and come on as a cop, or give him a ten-dollar bill and be the good guy. He looked as if he could use the money.

The rheumy gray eyes unclouded a bit as he took the bill with a shaking hand.

"I'm looking for Mr. Raymond Denko's apartment. I can't remember the number."

He scratched the top of his bald head. "Denko. That'd be apartment 635."

"He live alone?"

"Far as I know."

I thanked him and got in the elevator. For about ten seconds. The smell was enough to pickle herring. I needed the exercise anyway. The stairs didn't smell much better; it was as if every tenant had been cooking with old cabbage for the past ten years. Mix that with urine and unwashed bodies and you get the idea.

I took out the Magnum and used the butt to knock on the door of apartment 635. A radio was blaring out rock music from a nearby room. I waited, knocked again. Still nothing. I tested the door; it was locked. I tried to slip the lock the easy way, with a few old plastic calendars, but the wood had warped enough to make the door fit tight to the jamb.

Now the Boy and Girl Scouts of America have taught the country's youngsters wondrous things that can be done with a good knife. But not this trick. You need the Swiss

Army job, the one with all the gadgets. You have to modify the fish-scaling blade a little by grinding down some of the bumps, then you take out the metal tweezers. (Don't use the plastic toothpick, it'll break right off.) You insert the blade and start raking the tumblers, using the tweezers to hold them in place after they fall into their proper spring holes. This only works on simple warded locks or disc-tumbler locks. Anything more sophisticated and you have to go into a set of industrial safety picks. The beauty of the Swiss knife is that it cannot be easily classified by the police as a burglar tool. I raked and picked for less than a minute, then heard the satisfying click and the lock turned and the door opened.

Denko hadn't used the same decorator that Maya Price had. The floor was linoleumed in squares that were supposed to resemble bricks. A cracked vinyl chair sat alone in front of the curtained window. There was a small kitchen table with old newspapers as a tablecloth. A refrigerator wheezed noisily next to a sink, the porcelain stained a rusty brown. The bedroom was almost completely taken up by the unmade bed in the center of the room. A five-door bare pine bureau was crowded between the bed and a door that turned out to be a closet. It was stuffed with men's suits, sport coats, and shirts. The shirts had a locker-room smell to them.

Another door lead to the bathroom. The sink top had a can of shaving cream, a disposable razor, and a dirty washcloth on it. Sitting on top of the toilet bowl were a bottle of Old Spice after-shave and an old issue of *Playboy*.

The shower curtain was plastic, decorated in big bright yellow and red flowers. The curtain rings were rusty and made scraping noises as I slid the curtain back.

There sat Raymond Denko. Or rather, there lay Raymond Denko. His mouth was open wide, his tongue halfway out. His eyes looked surprised even in death. There were two bullet holes stitched right across his chest. The bottom of the shower was thick with his blood. He was naked. His hair was stiff and stuck together in ringlets, as if he'd been shampooing just before he was shot. A plastic bottle of Head and Shoulders lay by his feet. A plain white towel was draped over his knees. I picked it up carefully with two fingers. There was a hole in several places in the towel. Someone had wrapped it around the barrel of a gun to deaden the noise.

I took out a handkerchief, wiped the metal shower rings and slid them back. I took a quick check in the bedroom, running my hands through his suit and pants pockets. Nothing but some loose change and a couple of matchbooks.

The top drawer of the bureau held his wallet; just a few tens and six ones. His driver's license, a card from his parole officer, and a condom. There was a set of car keys on a chain with a rabbit's foot, something I hadn't seen in years, and, judging from Denko's luck, it was just as well.

The rest of the drawers were filled with underwear, both clean and dirty, socks, the usual stuff.

The kitchen cabinets held what kitchen cabinets are supposed to hold. The refrigerator had nothing but two six-packs of Bud Light beer. The trash can under the sink was filled with empty beer cans, a bottle of Andre's champagne, and a pint bottle of vodka.

I took a last look around, then went over to the kitchen table and leafed through the newspapers. They were old, and six deep. When one got dirty, Denko didn't throw it away, just covered it up with another paper. I remember being a uniformed cop and watching the ambulance attendants look under the kitchen-table papers when some poor old-timer passed away. It was a favorite hiding place. "The Irish safety-deposit box," they'd call it, and pocket the money quickly if you didn't watch them closely.

Denko had made pretty good use of his "Irish safety-deposit box." There were layers of bills, twenties and hundreds. I didn't bother to count them, just left them there, for the cops. Or the ambulance attendants.

14

There was a black-and-white police car parked in my driveway, the red light on the roof spinning slowly, the two front doors left open, as if the cops had been in a hurry when they hopped out.

There was no way that anyone could have found Denko's body and associated me with it that quickly. I had walked almost six blocks before picking up a cab, and had the cabbie drop me two blocks from my place. That took what? A half hour, forty minutes. No way. Still, my stomach was doing flip-flops as I walked up the steps to my flat. The front door was wide open, the lights on. A uniformed cop, young, still in his twenties, swung one of those big six-cell flashlights in my direction.

"Who are you?" he asked.

"Nick Polo. This is my place. What happened?"

"Somebody called in a 911. Couldn't speak English, from what the dispatcher said. We didn't know what we had."

Another officer, older, bigger, grumpier, came from the back of the flat. "You the owner?"

"Right."

"They did a job on you, buddy." He squinted his eyes. "Don't I know you?"

"I think we met a few times. My name's Polo. I used to be one of you."

He snapped two fingers as big as Polish sausages. They made a surprisingly small sound. "Yeah, Polo, right. Now I remember. We need to know what's missing. It looks like it might take you a while to figure that out."

He was right. The front room was a shambles. All the records had been pulled out of their holders and thrown around the floor. The backs and cushions on the couch had been slit, the stuffing spilling out like dough from a cake pan.

The kitchen was just as bad: pots, pans, canned goods littered the floor. I stepped on something crunchy. Coffee beans.

All the files had been removed from the office file cabinets and dumped on the floor. The desk's drawers were all open, most of the contents dumped on top of the file folders. The computer screen was on, the screen blank. The plastic holder where I kept all the floppy disks was empty. I checked the desk, moved a few of the folders with my feet. There was no sign of the mini recorder, and no sign of any of the cassettes, not the blank ones, nor the one I'd used to record my meeting with Maya Price.

The cabinet holding my cameras and electronic equipment was knocked over on its side, but nothing seemed to be missing. The bedroom was worse. The mat-

93

tress was slit apart like the front-room furniture. My suits and sport coats were thrown on top of the bed. I checked the linings of the coats. Most were slit open.

I flopped down onto the bed feeling sick, sorry for myself, and awfully pissed off. I was hoping that whoever had done this had had the decency not to dump my liquor down the sink, when something more important occurred to me.

"There's an old lady who lives downstairs. Mrs. Damonte. Have you spoken to her? Is she okay?"

The older cop shook his head and chuckled. "Yeah, she's all right. I talked to her. Or tried to talk to her. She was hot about something, but I don't know what it was; have to get a translator, I guess."

"I'll talk to her. Thanks, Officers, not much more you can do here. I'll make a list of what's missing and make a supplemental report tomorrow."

They took a few more notes: last time I left, any prior burglaries, any idea why anyone would do this; that kind of thing.

After they left, I took a look at what remained of the front door. No fancy lock picks had been used on this one. Just a big pry bar. There were deep gouges in the door frame. Noisy way to break in, but certainly effective.

While I was looking at the door, Mrs. Damonte came up to see me.

"I called the police when I saw your door," she said in Italian. "I didn't go inside."

"You did the right thing."

"I was not home. At a wake," she said almost apologetically.

"Just as well you weren't home. These were bad men."

She walked into my flat, her eyes widening as she saw the destruction.

"You want me to help you fix?"

"Yes, that would be nice. It's a big job, though."

"I have friends help." She clicked her tongue. "Have to pay them money."

"That's fine," I said.

She walked through the flat, shaking her head and mumbling. When she was back at the front door, she said one word. "Shita."

Amazing. She had doubled her command of the English language with just one word. Shita and nopa. Just the basics.

I closed the front door as best I could, putting a chair loaded with pots and pans in front of it. If someone was planning to come back, he'd have to make a lot of noise to get past it. The liquor was intact, so I helped myself to a semi-lethal dose of Jack Daniels, and then checked under the sink. They hadn't found the hiding place under the kitchen sink. The copies of the plans, along with the cash and family jewels, were still there. I slept in what remained of my bed, making sure the .357 Magnum was within easy reach.

Mrs. Damonte was there bright and early the next morning, with fresh-baked panettone—a light, sweet bread— and her troops, two happy-faced women in flower-print dresses named Florence and Carmen. They were spring chickens compared to Mrs. D; they couldn't have been more than seventy.

Mrs. D started giving out orders. Her two buddies started in the living room, she took the kitchen, and I got the office.

I stopped around ten to call my insurance company about the car. This time I got a live voice. An unhappy live voice. They promised to send an adjuster out that afternoon. I checked with the garage on the car; it was a total; the repair work would cost more than the car was worth.

My buddy at the robbery detail, Paul Paulsen, called.

"Nick. That guy you were in asking about yesterday. Denko? He was killed yesterday."

"Where at?"

"He had an apartment on Hyde Street. Shot two times. With a .38."

"Who's handling the case for homicide?"

"Tehaney."

"Did you tell him about me picking Denko out of the mug shots?"

"No."

And Paulsen wouldn't, but I didn't want to push a friendship too far. "Why don't you, Paul. Tehaney will probably want to talk to me about it."

"Yeah."

"Do you know what time this Denko was killed?"

"No, nothing solid from what I could find out. Sometime in the afternoon is what they've got now, until the autopsy comes in."

"Thanks, Paul. Tell Tehaney. And tell him I'll be at home all day if he wants to see me."

A locksmith came by, took one look at the door and declared that a total, also. Getting him to agree to putting in a new door and lock on a rush basis was like negotiating with the Russians on arms control, but eventually we got to the right price, and I was promised a door by the afternoon.

The morning went by quickly, interrupted by more insurance company calls. I took a coffee break and went to check on the ladies. They were refiling the records in their jackets and giggling like schoolgirls. I couldn't quite pick up everything they were saying, the dialect must have been from northern Italy, but Julio Iglesias' name popped up a couple of times.

Mrs. D had sorted out my clothes into those that she could fix, those that had to go to the tailor, and those that were beyond repair. We were negotiating her sewing fees when Inspector Bob Tehaney showed up.

"You lead an interesting life," he said as he surveyed the wreckage. "Somewhere we can talk?"

We settled on his car.

"Paul Paulsen tells me you picked a Raymond Denko out of the mug-shot files yesterday after you left my office."

"Right. I thought he might be the same guy who tried to mug me a while back."

"Mug you?"

"Right about there," I said, pointing to the steps leading to my flat. "It was the night after the poker game with Paul Randall, Ronald Dettman, and Allen Price."

"Why didn't you tell me about it?"

"I didn't think it had a connection, Bob. There's a lot of mugging going around now."

Tehaney crushed an empty pack of Lucky's, tossed it in the backseat, and patted his pocket for more. "You're not going to start getting cute on me now, are you, Nick?"

He split open the fresh pack with his fingernail and lit up. "I've got enough of these assholes playing cute on me in this case already."

"Tell me about Denko."

"Shot while he was in the shower. Twice. A .38. We're running the bullets now. Be interesting if it was the same gun that killed Price, wouldn't it?"

"Very. What time was he shot?"

"Between three in the afternoon and six in the evening yesterday."

"I was with Mrs. Maya Price in the afternoon yesterday, at her home in Belvedere. On the way back I got in a wreck on the Golden Gate Bridge. My car had to be towed. It didn't get to the garage until almost six."

"Somebody went to see Denko last night. Around nine. About your age and height. Slipped the manager ten bucks for the number to Denko's apartment."

"Denko was already dead by then, wasn't he?"

"Yeah. I'd still like to talk to this guy. Where were you around that time?"

"I had dinner in North Beach. Went to a few bars. Came home and found that someone had broken into my place and torn it apart."

"What were they looking for, Nick?"

"I wish I knew."

Tehaney rubbed the glowing end of his cigarette back and forth across the surface of the ashtray. "I wish I knew too. I'll let you know when we get the ballistic report back. If it is the same gun, we'll have to talk some more. What did Maya Price want to see you about?"

"She said that Price had some business papers with him the night he was killed. She wanted to hire me to find them."

"Business papers, eh? Funny, she never mentioned that to me. Of course a lot of people don't tell me things that they think are important to them. Things that they think a dumb cop wouldn't understand." Tehaney hit the car's ignition switch. The engine burst into life and the motor rose and fell as he played with the accelerator. "Did you tell her you'd take the job?"

"No," I said, easing out of the car's seat.

"And after you leave her place, you get into an accident and then your place is broken into. You do lead an exciting life, Nick. I couldn't handle it myself."

I watched until Tehaney's car disappeared down toward Columbus Avenue, then went back in to do battle with Mrs. D.

15

I stayed in the office the rest of the afternoon, trying to piece the files back together again. The loss of the floppy disks was going to be a problem. There were some items on the disks that could be embarrassing to the clients.

I stopped for a coffee break and watched as Mrs. D and her girls went about their work. An insurance adjuster came by, and I walked him through the damage.

Why so much damage? Sure, they were looking for the papers I'd taken from Dettman, but why go through all the trouble of cutting up my clothes? Ransacking the kitchen? It was overkill. Or maybe they were trying to cover up something. The little old light bulb went on over my head, and I went back to the office. I have two exotic-sounding little machines: The Hound Dog, and the Mark III Bug Catcher. Jazzy names for electronic instruments designed for the sole purpose of locating hidden transmitters.

Neat machines: small enough to hold in your hand,

accurate; the only problem is they run on batteries, and sure enough, the batteries were dead.

I hustled down to a nearby hardware store, loaded up the machines with nice fresh Duracells, and went to work. I've got four phones in the flat: front room, kitchen, bedroom, and office. Each had a microtransmitter, about the size of a postage stamp, stuck in the plastic terminal box connected to the phone's cord. Nice little things, they can work off the juice from the phone itself and are backed up with two mercury button batteries. Transmission distance could go a long way. Several blocks. With a strong-enough receiver, a man, say Mr. Dettman himself, could beam down on me from his apartment on Taylor Street and be treated to a day and a night in the life of Nick Polo.

I disconnected the bugs and used the Bug Catcher and Hound Dog to check out the rest of the flat. All clear. They had just tapped the telephones, and why not, they're the easiest places to plant a bug.

So far Dettman, or whoever the hell had been listening, hadn't really picked up much. There was the call from Paul Paulsen; Denko's name popped up in that conversation. The rest of the calls were to and from insurance people.

After I had dismantled the bugs, I did get three calls my electronic eavesdroppers would have been interested in: my stockbroker called, suggesting that I buy some more of Dettman Industries. It had gone up four points since I bought it, and the word on the street was that a takeover bid could push it a lot higher. Four points, five hundred shares; so I'd made something like two thousand bucks so far. No sense getting greedy, either in poker or

101

the market, so I instructed him to put in a sell order if it went up another two points.

Alicia Dettman called all out of breath and excited. Ron hadn't been home in two nights, and she couldn't get ahold of him at his plant. She wanted to come right over. I told her the situation, and she volunteered to bring dinner over around seven. Judging from the state of my kitchen, it was an offer I couldn't refuse.

Bob Tehaney called to let me know that the bullet that killed Mr. Raymond Denko did not come from the same gun that killed Allen Price. Surprise, surprise. Tehaney also mentioned that he hadn't been able to make contact with Ronald Dettman. I told him about Janet Drew's apartment on Taylor Street.

"Janet Drew," he said. "That's a new name to me."

So far, Janet Drew was a lady of mystery to me also. I'd never even seen the woman, something I hoped to change by tomorrow.

The place looked reasonably clean by the time Alicia Dettman showed up. She waved her car keys in front of me.

"Everything's in the trunk," she said.

The Alfa's little trunk was jammed with white boxes labeled "Chaput's Caterers," which had steam coming out from them. They turned out to be full of all kinds of goodies: escargots, cream of avocado soup, a shrimp quiche, two small roast ducks in orange sauce, and a choc-olate-rum cake with enough calories to turn Twiggy into a Richard Simmons candidate overnight.

I tucked the Alfa in the garage after emptying the trunk. Alicia wandered around the flat with a martini in her hands. "Did they steal anything?" she asked.

"No, just tore things apart."

"Do you think Ron was responsible?" She was dressed in red this time, pants and a safari-style blouse with epaulets, flaps, and all kinds of tiny little pockets that had no real use whatsoever. She had gold bracelets on each arm that jangled when she moved.

"Do you?" I asked, starting to sort out the caterer's boxes.

"I think he's capable of anything, Nick."

I poured the soup into a pot, put the ducks in a Corning Ware casserole, and got the stove going. "Did you ever hear Ron mention the name Ray Denko?"

Her face seemed to freeze for a moment. "Denko. No. I don't think so, why?"

"I think he was a business associate of your husband's. He was murdered yesterday."

She shrugged those elegant shoulders. "Ron has so many business associates. What kind of work did this Denko do?"

"He robbed people."

She laughed, poured more gin into her glass, and handed me a drink. "There are lots of ways to rob people, Nick. Lots of ways."

"This guy was old-fashioned. Stuck a gun into your ribs and took whatever you had."

We started with the escargots and worked our way through the rest of the meal. "My compliments to your caterer," I said, tipping over the end of a bottle of champagne.

She had brandy while I tried a slice of the chocolate cake.

"The night I first met you, you mentioned that Ron

was always giving envelopes stuffed with money to people. Why?" I asked between mouthfuls of the obscenely delicious cake.

"There's a lot of under-the-table dealing in the electronic business."

"Would Ron be buying his competitors' secrets?"

She put her hand under her chin and pouted. "He always kept me in the dark about what went on in his business. He thought I was just too bubble-headed to understand what was going on. But he passed around a lot of cash, I know that. Not to me, but we'd be at a party and I'd see him hand over some money, or people would come to the house, like you did, and there would be a nicely stuffed envelope waiting for them."

"Have you ever heard the name Janet Drew?"

Her eyes narrowed. "Drew? No. Why? Is she one of his girls? He's had several. I haven't been able to keep up with all of them."

"It's just a name that popped into the investigation. I met with the Dragon Lady yesterday."

"You did? Maya Price? What did you think of her?"

"She doesn't seem to be mourning too heavily over poor old Al's death. She wanted to hire me. She said that something was stolen from Al's car the night he was killed. Some papers he'd gotten from your husband."

She stood up, walked over to the kitchen counter, and came back with the brandy bottle, poured me a glass and topped off hers.

"Papers? What kind of papers?"

"Something to do with a project Ron was working on. Neurocomputing."

"When I hear words like that, I'm glad I don't know

104

too much about the business." Her tongue darted out, imparting a moist sheen to her lips. "Have you found out anything yet about what we talked about? About getting something on Ron that'll get me out of this mess?"

"No, but I'm working on it. I was checking court records on your husband. The divorce action you filed a couple of years ago showed up."

"That was a disaster. His attorneys chewed my attorney to pieces. That's when I found out just how tight a box he's got me wrapped up in."

She walked over and sat in my lap. Her tongue started working on my ear. It didn't need much work. I unbuttoned her blouse just far enough so I could see her bra. It was red, lacy, thin as tracing paper, and had one of mankind's all-time great inventions: front hooks. It unsnapped at a touch. Her nipples were hard as buttons. She took her tongue out of my ear and ran it down to the hollow of my throat. "Mmmmmmmm," she purred, like a cat. We disentangled long enough to make it to the bedroom.

16

Alicia left before midnight, so by eight the next morning I was up, showered, shaved, and stuffed with panettone and leftover duck.

I tried calling Dettman at Janet Drew's number. There was no answer.

My insurance company, in gratitude for seven years of loyal payments without a claim, was allowing me a rental car for three full days. The super-econo rental, at fourteen bucks a day. I up-up-upgraded all the way to a Lincoln Continental coupe and drove down to Harrison Street, to Larsen's Electronics.

Bill Larsen, the owner, was a tall, thin guy with hair the color of chrome. He had enough goodies in the back of his shop to supply the CIA and FBI for years.

I showed him the bugs I'd taken from my phone.

"Cheap," he said. "Cheap, but effective."

"I need a receiver that can work with these."

"You want top quality, I take it."

"I want to rent whatever you've got available that is nice and simple to use and will carry for a couple of blocks."

"Are you going to be in a car?"

"No, a house."

Knowing from past experience that my solution to repairing any electronic device that wasn't functioning properly was to hit it with a hammer, and, if that didn't work, look for a bigger hammer, Larsen went into some detailed technical explanations of the materials he was renting me: UHF/VHF amplifier, and booster antenna. By the time I left his shop I felt reasonably confident that I could handle the job. Then I saw a bad omen: a traffic tag flopping under the recessed windshield wipers of the Lincoln.

I used a pay phone to try and reach Dettman again. Still no answer. I then stopped at a library, checked the reverse address for 1777 Taylor, wrote down several names, and went in search of a phone booth.

Still no answer at Janet Drew's number. I went down the phone list for 1777 Taylor, and got a response from a Mrs. Fielder, in apartment 903.

"Yes, Mrs. Fielder, this is Don Taylor at the water department. We received some complaints from the people in your building regarding water pressure. Are you having any trouble?"

"I don't think so, young man; let me check," she said.

And check she did. Apparently every faucet in the place, because she didn't come back on the line for almost five minutes.

"Everything is working perfectly," she said finally.

"Fine, Mrs. Fielder. We'll be running some tests today, so if you have any problems, just call us. Will you be in most of the day?"

"Yes, I will. We've never had a problem with the water here."

"Well, thanks for your cooperation, ma'am, and have a drink on me."

I stopped at a florist, keeping a nervous eye on the Lincoln in a red zone, while the man made me up a forty-dollar bouquet.

The daytime security guard at Janet Drew's building was wearing gray slacks and a blue blazer, just like my Chicago cop friend had. He was a short, thin guy with a long narrow nose and a graying mustache.

He gave me the kind of smile they reserve for people in Rolls, Cads, and Lincolns.

"Good morning," I said, slipping him a twenty-dollar bill. I held up the flowers and smiled. "It's Auntie Ellen's birthday. I want to surprise her."

"Auntie Ellen?"

"Fielder. It's her birthday today. How old do you think she is?"

He scratched his head. "Jeez, mister, I couldn't say . . ."

"Good idea. She's touchy as hell about it." I walked confidently to the door. "Don't buzz her, I want this to be a surprise."

He hesitated for just a beat, then smiled and pushed the button that released the door. "Nice lady, Mrs. Fielder. Tell her happy birthday for me."

I knocked loudly on Janet Drew's door. Nothing. Then went to work with the Swiss Army knife. The building hadn't wasted much money on security with the door locks. After all, why should they? They had a guard at the front entrance.

There was just one bedroom, but it was big. King-sized bed, covered in dark blue silk. The furniture was bleached walnut. There was a picture of a beautiful woman on a dresser. Her head was tilted, eyes slightly arched, seemingly flirting with the camera. I studied it for several seconds. So far that was as close as I'd gotten to Janet Drew. The phone was modern, in molded plastic, designed like a half-moon. I followed the cord to the junction box, which was behind the bed's end table, opened it up with a screwdriver from the Swiss Army knife, and guess what I found. A bug. Exactly like the ones in my pocket. Coming out of the box were a pair of thin wires, painted the same cream color as the wall. The wires disappeared behind the baseboard. I pried the board up and followed the wires several feet, to just about under the middle of the bed. There were several Gucci shoe boxes there. I pulled out the one the wires went into and found a Sony cassette recorder. It was a good recorder, voice-activated, battery-operated, big enough to handle cassettes of ninety minutes on each side. I disconnected the lines from the phone and punched the "rewind" button. The tape whisked back for a few seconds, and I pushed the "play" button. There were the sounds of footsteps, and someone whistling "I've Got You Under My Skin." It took me a couple of seconds to realize I was listening to my own feeble efforts. There was the sound of furniture being moved and the scraping noise from my screwdriver. There was no "erase" button on the machine. You didn't erase a tape, you simply rewound it and played over it. I

109

pushed the "fast-forward" button so the cassette went to the end, then reversed it so that the opposite side of the cassette was now in position. I pushed the "play" button again. This side of the tape was blank.

I checked the phones in the front room and kitchen. They were bugged too. I didn't spend much time with them. They were probably all hooked up in series so the recorder under the bed picked them all up.

I would have loved to take my time and go through the place thoroughly, but the doorman might start getting nervous and call up good old Auntie Ellen. I went back to the bedroom and carefully reconnected the wires from the phone's junction box to the cassette recorder, then exited as quietly as I could. I took the elevator to the ninth floor and knocked on the door for 903.

A short, smiling woman in her seventies opened the door.

I handed her the bouquet of flowers. "From the water company, ma'am. Thanks for your help."

17

I drove back to my flat and, feeling slightly paranoid, checked the telephones for bugs again. They were clear, and I called Dettman's office. He was once again "unavailable." I called his house. The maid told me that both Mr. and Mrs. Dettman were out.

What the hell was Dettman up to? Bugging my place made sense. But why the apartment? Didn't he trust the mysterious Janet Drew? Alicia said he had tape recordings of her and her playmates. Was he doing the same thing with Drew? Was that how he got his kicks? Or was Drew the one who set up the bugs? If so, why? She could bug her own place easily enough, but the bugs were duplicates of the ones used on my flat. Why the hell would she have any reason to bug me?

I called Bob Tehaney.

"Did you get to interview Janet Drew, Bob?"

"Yep. Wasn't much of an interview."

"What's she like?"

111

"Smart. Cold. Very lovely young lady."

"What did she say about Dettman?"

He laughed. "It's what she didn't say about Dettman. She answers every question with the least words possible, as if they were worth money and she didn't want to spend them. She and Dettman are good friends. She claims she met Price through Dettman, had just a nodding acquaintance with him. Said she never heard of anyone called Raymond Denko."

"What about Dettman?"

"I'm having trouble getting to him. All I ever get is his secretary."

"I know the feeling."

"I did talk to Maya Price again. She says that you must have been mistaken. Says that she never told you that her husband had any valuable papers of any kind on him when he was killed. Says you came over to shake her down, tried to get her to pay you to find out who did kill her husband."

"Nice lady."

"Keep in touch, Nick," he said.

"Damn it," I said after hanging up the phone with more force than necessary. Good old Maya Price. Now *there* was a lady whose phone I'd love to bug. I leaned back in the swivel chair to that point of balance where, if you go back another notch, it'll tip over, and stared at the ceiling. Dettman. Where the hell was he? Think, Polo. You're a detective. Start detecting. Not exactly a Knute Rockne pep talk, but it got the little gray cells churning in my confused brain. Where the hell would Dettman be? With Drew? Out of town? I looked out the window. It was a bright, beautiful, sunny day. A nice day for sailing, swimming. And golf. Why not golf? I looked up the number for the St. Francis Golf Club.

"Hello. I'm supposed to play with Mr. Dettman today, but I forgot the starting time."

I heard the rustling of papers. "His tee time is one-thirty, sir."

I thanked the nice young man, changed into casual slacks, sport shirt and a sweater, went to the garage and threw my clubs in the back of the Lincoln and drove south. Not very far south. The St. Francis Golf Club is located just on the San Francisco–Daly City border. I had played there years ago when they used to let the police department play the course on Mondays, when it was closed to the members for maintenance. It was a beautiful course: long, rolling fairways, enough sand traps to make Lawrence of Arabia feel at home. Tall, majestic pines and eucalyptus trees narrowed the fairways. The club had a membership of just a couple of hundred, and the only way to get in was if one of the members died and opened a spot.

I parked near the clubhouse, a two-story Tudor affair with a steep slate roof and arched dormers. I got my putter, rummaged through the bag and found three fairly decent balls, and strolled to the practice putting green, which was situated between the clubhouse, caddy shack, and first tee. It was twenty minutes until Dettman was due to tee off. I rolled my putts, getting a feel for the speed and the breaks caused by the undulating greens. I was working hard on a four-footer when a large shadow suddenly fell across my golf ball.

"What the fuck do you think you're doing here?" asked Ronald Dettman between clenched teeth.

"I just thought I'd give you a chance to get some of your money back. What say we have a little putting contest? A hundred bucks a hole?"

Dettman looked as if he was going to take a swing at me at first, then he gave a tambourine laugh and said, "Don't go away. I'll be right back."

He walked toward the caddy shack, waving his right hand in the air. A caddy who looked old enough to be courting Mrs. Damonte ran over with Dettman's bag. He pulled his putter from the bag as if it were Excalibur from the rock.

"You've got guts, I'll say that for you, Polo," Dettman said, dropping an orange ball alongside my white one. "You go first," he said, gesturing to a hole some twenty-five feet away.

I stroked the ball, and it went sliding past the hole some five feet.

Dettman's ball rimmed the cup, stopping just inches past it. I missed my five-footer coming back.

"That's one hundred," he said, immediately lining up his next putt, which once again rimmed the hole. Again mine went well past the cup and again I missed the comeback putt.

"That's two hundred, Polo. You really should stick to what you know."

I waited until he putted again, this time two feet short of the hole. "What do you know about someone breaking into my place the other night and tearing it apart?"

"Not a thing," he said, watching my putt go way past the hole again. This time I made the second putt. He tapped his in nonchalantly with one hand. "I've got a game in a few minutes. What say we double the stakes and get this over with?"

"Okay. Five more holes, at two hundred each, then we call it quits."

"Done." His putt was a little strong this time. Mine went right into the center of the cup.

"Not only did someone break into my place, they planted some bugs in the telephone." This time my putt was hole-high, just a few inches to the left.

"I know nothing about any of this." He was strong again. A good four feet away. He took his time over his second putt, then pulled it to the right. My hole.

"Where did you learn to play golf?" Dettman asked.

"Lompoc Federal Prison. I was the greens keeper. Not much of a course, but it had a beautiful putting green. The warden was an avid golfer."

The next cup was no more than twelve feet away and I drilled mine right into the hole again. Dettman's ball hit the hole, bouncing up in the air and spinning some five feet away.

"I thought someone in your business would be very familiar with electronic eavesdropping devices, Dettman."

He jingled some change in his pocket just about the same time my putter made contact with the ball. The hole was about forty-five feet away this time, and I came up a few feet short.

Dettman's ball was short too, but a good foot inside mine. My second putt hit the side of the hole, spun completely around it, then dropped safely into the bottom of the cup.

"Lucky bastard," Dettman said, lining up his shot.

"Where's Janet Drew?" I asked as he was about to putt.

He looked up at me like a botanist confronting an unknown species, then hit his putt. The ball stopped on the edge of the hole, hanging there, trying to make up its mind whether to drop into the hole or not. It stayed there. Dettman walked up and slammed his foot down by the hole, trying to get the ball to move. When it didn't he kicked it away.

"I think that makes it four to zero, Ronnie. Last hole coming up." I took my time lining up the final putt. The hole was some fifteen feet away, on the edge of a slope. "I was checking court records and found out that your wife tried divorcing you a couple of years ago. I'm surprised you didn't let her go. Or didn't you know Janet Drew then?"

"Shut up and putt, you miserable fucker!"

A group of three men had gathered around the putting green. They were all prosperous-looking middle-aged gentlemen dressed in nicely matched cashmere sweaters and polyester pants. One of them called out, "Ron, we're due on the first tee."

My putt went up the slope, took the drop and hit the hole and dropped in. If it hadn't hit the hole it would have probably rolled all the way off the green.

Dettman didn't even bother putting. He reached angrily into his pants pocket, pulled out a money clip, and handed me eight crisp hundred-dollar bills. "If I ever see you again, I'll kill you, you rotten bastard."

"Tell Janet I'd like to talk to her," I said. Then, when Dettman was with his group of friends and I was walking back to my car, I turned around and yelled, "Oh,

Ron. By the way. Inspector Tehaney of the San Francisco Police Department has been trying to get ahold of you. Have a nice round."

He kept his back to me and didn't respond, but his shoulders hunched up and his neck went down, like a turtle ducking back into his shell. I wished I could have seen his face.

18

I checked the Lincoln's rearview mirror a dozen times as I drove back into town. If someone was following me, he was a real pro, because I couldn't spot him. I made a quick stop at the Hall of Justice. Bob Tehaney was behind his desk.

"If you're still interested in seeing Ron Dettman, you can catch him at the St. Francis Golf Club. He should be out on the course for another couple of hours."

"Thanks." Tehaney sucked on his ever-present cigarette. "The autopsy on Raymond Denko came in. Not much of interest, except his blood alcohol was fourteen percent, so at least he went out of this cruel world with a heat on." He waded through some papers on his desk, then looked up at me. "You've already seen his rap sheet, haven't you? He was working as a bartender. At Ferrando's."

"On Sixteenth Street?"

"Right. Worked the swing shift."

Ferrando's was a working-man's bar in the Potrero District. At one time it was a big money maker, being situated right across the street from Seals Stadium, where the minor-league San Francisco Seals baseball team played, and later, the Giants, until the wise city fathers, and some suddenly wealthy landowners and contractors, decided on building a new stadium, Candlestick Park, on a site by the bay that rivaled the Arctic Circle in weather conditions.

There was a ticket stuck on the Lincoln's windshield when I got back onto the street. I drove home. The phone rang as soon as I was in the door.

"Mr. Polo. This is Maya Price. I'm disappointed in you. I thought we had an understanding."

"An understanding about what?"

"You told Inspector Tehaney about those reports."

"Well, I was a little disappointed in you, Maya. Seems that after I left your house the other day, someone tried running me off the bridge."

There was a pause of several seconds. "You do not seriously think that I would attempt something like that?"

"It could be a coincidence, but coincidences scare the hell out of me."

"I assure you, Mr. Polo, that your good health is to my advantage. I would like to talk to you again. Today. It is very important."

"I'm kind of booked up—"

"And profitable, Mr. Polo. Very profitable."

She struck my greed button. "Are you at home now?"

"Yes."

119

"What say we meet in an hour. Do you know where the Java House is on Embarcadero?"

"I will find it."

She severed the connection before I had a chance to say anything else.

I made a quick change into a sport coat that could hide the .357 Magnum, picked up a pair of binoculars, then drove right down to the Embarcadero, which is a fancy name for a street that hugs the bay from Pier 44 north to Fisherman's Wharf. The piers south of the Ferry Building are mostly rotting, creosote-soaked fire hazards. The Java House is a coffee shop snuggled right up against the water. I parked two blocks away, then walked to the restaurant, got a cup of coffee to go, and, shooing away pigeons and sea gulls, leaned against a decaying post and waited. It should take Maya Price another half hour to drive from Belvedere. She'd have to drive right past the spot where her husband was shot.

The sun was shining brightly, and if it hadn't been for the Magnum, I would have taken off my coat and enjoyed the day. Two youngsters, not yet in their teens, had their legs draped over the pier, fishing. About every five minutes they would reel in a fat, oily-looking perch.

"Wanna buy a fish?" one of the kids asked.

"No, thanks." He was a bright-looking kid, all blue eyes, freckles, and blond hair. Norman Rockwell would have found him a model model. "Hey, kid. You fish here often?"

"Yeah."

"You ever eat what you catch?"

"You kiddin'? If we can't sell 'em, we throw 'em back. I wouldn't eat nothin' that comes out of that water."

Wise beyond his years. He and his buddy bagged another half dozen fish by the time a dark maroon Aston Martin Lagonda pulled into the lot in front of the Java House. I watched her through the binoculars. She sat perfectly still, her face devoid of expression. I kept an eye on her for a couple of minutes. No one pulled in behind her. She got out of the car, looked around, then entered the coffeehouse. She was the type who would get fast service no matter where she went, and the Java House was no exception. She was sitting at a table, a large steaming white mug of coffee in front of her, by the time I got there.

She was dressed in maroon this time: coat, slacks, scarf, even the lenses of her sunglasses. The same color as her car. I wondered if she had a car for each outfit. She placed a dollar bill next to her untouched coffee cup. "Let's walk," she said.

We strolled at a slow pace.

"I made you an offer of twenty-five thousand dollars for copies of the papers you took from Ronald Dettman. Did you find someone who would pay you more?"

"I told you I didn't have the papers."

"Someone did. They have been sold."

"How do you know?"

She stopped, took off her sunglasses and pinched the bridge of her nose. "There are several parties who were very anxious to get their hands on those papers. But suddenly there is one less interested party. Because they now have them. If it wasn't you that sold them, then it was the person who killed my husband."

"What about Dettman? Maybe he sold them."

"Not possible, Mr. Polo. Ronald Dettman needs those papers. He needs them exclusively."

"That doesn't seem possible now, does it?"

She put her glasses back on and turned back toward her car. "No, it doesn't. I'm prepared to up my offer to fifty thousand dollars."

"What's so damn important about the papers? Dettman has the originals. I gave them to him. That puts him in control, doesn't it?"

She stopped at the Aston Martin, waiting for me to open the door. "He's only in control if he can put the technology to use before someone else does," she said, sliding in under the steering wheel.

"How can you be so sure your husband had the papers?"

"My husband and I did not have what you might call a conventional marriage. But we did communicate. Especially when it concerned business. He had certain connections. I have certain connections. He told me that he was definitely going to have copies of those specific documents that night. The night he was murdered. He said he was going to have physical possession of them. I had already contacted an interested party when I learned of my husband's death."

"Who did your husband get the papers from?"

The car's door closed with that thunk sound that seems to be standard equipment for any car costing over fifty thousand dollars.

She pushed a button and the window whispered down. "I don't know who Allen was dealing with. Be careful, Mr. Polo, and think seriously about my offer."

19

"Neurocomputing is simply a new form of silicone chips molded after the human nervous system," said Tim Fetzer.

Fetzer, who, according to my stockbroker, was the number-one expert on what's new in what he called the "technology sector of the market," saw the puzzled look on my face. I sipped at my drink and waved an arm at the bartender for another round. We were sitting on stools at a gin mill called The Office, which was situated within walking distance of the Stock Exchange.

"What they're doing," continued Fetzer, in a soft, professional voice, "is studying the nervous system of laboratory rats, dogs, monkeys—hell, somewhere they're no doubt using human guinea pigs, too. Right now, computers work at lightning speed, but they still work on a sequence of individual instructions. It's like they fed a problem into one of your ears and it had to pass through your entire body before the information hit your brain, then the brain would have to process the information, then ship it out. A neurochip would eliminate all those extra steps."

"And that's good, huh?" I said, dropping a five-dollar bill on the bar and picking up a fresh drink.

Fetzer looked to be in his late thirties, with thinning brown hair worn long and shaggy and a bushy mustache that drooped down halfway to his chin. He picked up his drink, tequila over ice, took a sip, then said, "Good? It would make everything we have now obsolete. There's no limit to what these babies will be able to do. They'll be able to instantly recognize shapes, colors, horizons. A whole new world will open up to the scientists, and they'll let it trickle out, piece by piece, in the form of new medicines, new products, new bombs—you name it."

"And just when will these chips be available?"

Fetzer shrugged his shoulders. "Who knows? It could be next year, it could be twenty years from now. I'll tell you one thing, though. Whoever comes out with the first neurochip that really performs well is going to make a fortune.

"Any rumors on the street about who is doing what?"

"No, not really. Research is going on all over the world. If I knew who'd be first, I'd sell the house and everything else and start buying stock right now."

I thanked Fetzer for his information and walked out to Kearny Street, and there it was, still another ticket on the Lincoln.

I'd had about enough. What's the old saying? When the going gets tough, the tough go shopping. I tried three

124

car dealers before I found the beauty I wanted, another slightly battered three-year-old Ford. This one was gray. By now it was after six and the body shop was closed, but the salesman promised that he could have a whip antenna installed for me in an hour if we closed the deal right then. I drove the Lincoln back to Hertz and cabbed it back in time to pick up the Ford. It still needed some work, but nothing that a little neglect and a half hour of parking in a Safeway lot wouldn't cure. I parked at the Marina Safeway, which, along with being one of the city's largest supermarkets, is also a renowned yuppie pickup spot. Love among the produce. I walked one block to Mulhearn's restaurant and sat alone over a dinner of sautéed prawns, trying to figure out just what the hell was going on.

In my dad's vault was a set of documents that Maya Price would give me fifty thousand dollars for. Yet I had no intention of selling the papers to her. Why not? Good question. I had come by them illegally, of course. And while the lessons the Good Sisters had pounded into me at grammar school didn't seem to have any effect on my love life, stealing was something else. Dettman had paid me for the damn things, and the only reason I'd kept the copies was for protection. And what about Dettman? Where did he get the papers? From his own plant, the product of his own, or his employees', sweat and blood? Or had he bought them from someone else? Alicia said he was always giving away envelopes stuffed with money, and knowing Dettman, I didn't think they were charitable contributions.

Somehow Allen Price got a copy. At least that's what Maya says. And that's why he was killed. So whoever killed Price sells the copies to one of those mysterious customers of Maya's. But how does Price's death tie in with Ray Denko's shooting? I paid for dinner, then walked back to the Safeway lot. I wasn't disappointed. There were two fresh dings on the driver's-side door.

Ferrando's Bar was half filled. The guy behind the plank was good-looking, with dark curly hair and the moves of an ex-athlete. I ordered a bourbon and water. This was not the kind of place where you ordered a silver fizz or Cherry Herring on the rocks. Shots, highballs, and beer. A jukebox was playing vintage Sinatra. The majority of the customers were middle-aged men, dressed in Levi's, cords, shirts with name tags sewn on. Teamsters, carpenters, bread drivers. A working-man's bar. I put down a twenty when my drink came.

"I wanted to ask you a few questions about Ray Denko."

"You a cop?"

"Used to be."

"Then what's Ray to you?"

"A few days ago he mugged me. Took something of value from me."

"Shit, you kidding me, man?"

"Nope."

He took my twenty, rang up the drink, then came back with the change.

"What's your name, buddy?"

"Polo, Nick Polo."

"*Paisan*, eh?"

"Sicilian."

"No shit. Sicilian. Bad people to cross."

126

"What kind of a guy was Denko?"

"A thief. A no-good goddamned thief," he said in a voice tuned by cigarettes and whiskey and not enough sleep.

"Why'd you let him work for you?"

Somebody called out, "Hey, Johnny," from the other end of the bar, and he went down to serve him. There were four men standing around a dark-haired girl on a stool. She had four untouched drinks stacked up in front of her. I sipped at mine and waited for the bartender to come back.

"You asked me why I let the bum work for me?" he asked, coming back with a drink I hadn't ordered. "He was my brother-in-law, that's why. My wife's brother. Shit. Let me tell you, my Sicilian friend, in this business you expect your bartenders to cheat on you. It's part of the game; you figure it into your operating expenses. But Ray, he was a fucking pig, man. He made more money on some of his shifts than I did. He wasn't even smart about it. I tried to help the bastard out and he steals me blind." He took two dollars from the change on the bar in front of me and rang it up on the cash register, then walked down and poured some more drinks for the other customers. He seemed to pour without being asked. If you only had two full drinks parked in front of you, he figured you were running on empty.

"What did Ray take from you?" he asked when he came back with another drink for me.

"A few bucks."

He hitched up his pants and cursed again. "Bastard. Thief. Horse player. And women. A real cunt hound. And for some reason they seemed to go for the big ugly bas-

127

tard. I could never figure it out. Not much I can tell you, *paisan*. Until he got killed I just worked the day shift. Now I got to put in a double shift. I don't know what the bastard did when he wasn't behind the plank. All I know is he stole me blind. Shit, man. Let me get you another drink."

20

I picked up what was left of the change from my twenty and went to the phone booth and called the Janet Drew number. Dettman answered. He sounded angry.

I put three fingers alongside my carotid artery and lowered my voice. "Hi. Is Janet there?"

"No. Who is this?"

"Just a friend," I said, then hung up.

My new beauty was safely and serenely parked in front of a fire hydrant, blessedly free of traffic tags. I drove over and parked across the street from 1777 Taylor Street. The doorman was new to me. A tall, skinny guy. I turned off the motor, leaned back and waited. Three cars drove into the courtyard, but Janet Drew wasn't in them. Shortly after eleven a silver Mercedes drove out. Dettman was at the wheel. His face looked grim and determined.

I drove around until I found a pay phone. If I ever did decide to sell those plans to Maya Price, the first thing I was going to buy was a car phone. I dialed Drew's number. No answer. Now how the hell was I going to get into the apartment again? The flowers for my auntie wouldn't work this time. I weighed the possibilities, then dialed 911.

"Police emergency."

You have to be careful with 911. The operator can tell just what number you're calling from, and they record all the calls.

I put my finger on my throat again and said, "This is 1777 Taylor. Apartment number 1401. There's been a shooting. I think she's still alive, but you better hurry."

I coud hear the sirens as I drove back to Taylor Street. Two radio cars and an ambulance. They were there almost twenty minutes. The ambulance left first, then the two police cars. I waited another five minutes, then drove in.

The security guard rushed out to greet me. I flashed him my badge.

"The black-and-whites gone already?" I asked in a gruff voice.

"Yes, sir. They didn't find nothing. Nothing at all. Must have been some kind of a crank."

"I better check it out just to make sure. Show me the way."

He lead me to the elevator and used his passkey to open the door to Drew's apartment.

"Where's the tenant?" I asked.

"Name's Janet Drew. She's out of town, Inspector. I think her mother got sick or something." He snapped on the lights.

"Okay, you can go back to your station. If this is a nut calling in, no telling what he'll do next."

130

The guard rubbed a long finger behind his ear, as if checking it out for dirt. "Yea, I guess you're right. Lots of nuts running around nowadays."

I waited until I heard the elevator start down, then went to the bedroom, reached under the bed and dragged out the Gucci box with the recorder. It was activated. The cassette showed some ten minutes of recording time. I pocketed the tape and took a quick look around the room. The bed was unwrinkled; there was a white wicker laundry basket against the far wall. It was empty. The front-room table by the phone had a half-filled cup of coffee on it. The ashtray was holding the remains of a cigar. I wondered if Dettman was coming back.

The security guard came out and held my car door open for me.

"Find anything, Inspector?"

"No. Just a nut, I guess. There was a cigar in the ashtray. I hope one of my men didn't leave it there."

He bulged his lower lip with his tongue. "Ah, no, I don't think it was your men. Ms. Drew has a gentleman friend who has a key. Must have been him."

"Must have." I switched on the ignition and nursed the motor to life. "Give us a call anytime you need us."

He gave me a semi-salute as I drove away.

21

I drove back to my flat and put the cassette into the stereo. At first the sounds were undistinguishable—movement noises of some type; walking, doors opening or closing—then the chirping noises of a push-button phone. A lot of chirps. I counted thirteen.

A feminine voice said something that sounded like "Mabuto" something-or-other.

Then Dettman's voice.

"Mr. Yamato, please."

"Who may I say is calling, sir?"

"Mr. Mercer."

There was nothing but the sound of static for a few seconds, then:

"Ah, Mr. Mercer. Where are you now?"

"Number three."

"Fifteen minutes."

There was a clatter as Dettman hung up the phone, then some more of those movement noises; some sounded like the clinking of ice against a glass.

Then came the throaty, ringing sound from the recorder picking up an incoming call.

"Dettman."

"Good evening, Mr. Dettman. Is it still evening in San Francisco?" It was Yamato's voice.

"A little later than that. How are things going?"

"Very well. Too well for your interests, perhaps."

"What do you mean?"

"Have you heard of a Dr. Rudolph Simpson?"

"No."

"He is a neurobiologist. He has been working with the top research team. They have set him up with his own laboratory. He has developed some extremely interesting ideas from working with the brains of rats. They seem to think that the information he is developing can help push the project ahead by a year or two."

"Shit," said Dettman. "Why didn't you tell me about this Simpson guy before?"

"I had no idea of his importance. Just a man in a laboratory with hundreds of rats. It could have meant anything."

"How much of his material can you get?"

"I could obtain copies of all he has done to date."

"And his feedback with the research team?"

"Yes."

"How much?"

"Since the risks are twice as high in obtaining this material, the cost will have to be twice as much as last time."

"A half million dollars?"

"That is correct."

"Can you guarantee that it will be worth that to me?"

"There are no guarantees in this world, Mr. Dettman, but you were satisfied with the other materials, weren't you?"

"Yes. I was satisfied. When can I get the information?"

"It is not wise for me to leave Japan for the next few weeks."

"Too long. I'll come to you. How soon?"

"Two days' time should be sufficient."

"Good. I'll confirm with you tomorrow."

"It will be better if you contact me at my home. You have the number?"

"Yes. Good-bye, Mr. Yamato."

There was the sound of another call being made by Dettman.

A sleepy voice answered.

"Yes. Who is it?"

"Dettman. I need a quick loan. A half million dollars. I need it in cash tomorrow."

"My God, Ron. Are you mad? Calling me up at this time to talk about a half million dollars."

I recognized the sleepy voice now. Paul Randall.

"I need the money right away, Paul."

"But Ron, you know that you're already—"

"Cut out the shit. Just get me the money. Use the house for collateral, one of the Industries buildings, whatever; just get me the money."

"I don't like being called—"

"And I don't like some pompous old bastard like you fucking my wife, Paul. And I bet your wife wouldn't much like it either. Is she there? Put her on the phone and I'll tell her about our mutual problem. And another thing I don't like is your friend Polo. You brought the

134

asshole to the club, had him cheat me at cards. Then he stole from me, blackmailed me. Even showed up at the golf course yesterday, threatened me again. And it's your fault, you stupid son of a bitch. Now get me the money by tomorrow!"

There was a crashing sound that made me wince as Dettman hung up the phone.

More movement, then another phone call. Ten chirps this time, so it was long distance.

"Hello?" The voice was soft, ladylike.

Dettman's voice had calmed down too.

"Is Janet there?"

"Just a minute. I'll get her."

"Ron?"

"Hi. How's your sister?"

"Oh, so-so. She's going to have to take a series of chemotherapy treatments. That's never very pleasant."

"How's the weather in LA?"

"Hot. I miss you."

"Same here. When are you coming back?"

"Tomorrow. I'm coming in on United. I'll get in around noon."

"Want me to have someone pick you up at the airport?"

"No. I'll take a cab. It's easier, and I can stop and do some shopping."

"Okay, we'll make a night of it tomorrow. Then I'll have to go to Tokyo for a day or two. Say hello to your sister for me."

Janet Drew's voice turned husky. "I look forward to tomorrow night. Sleep warm, darling."

There was a little more of those movements sounds, then a door slamming, then silence.

I rewound the cassette, put in the stereo's dubber and made a copy, then flopped back into my chair and tried to figure out just what the hell I had there.

Dettman was busy buying out his competitors' secrets. Maybe the boy genius wasn't such a genius after all. Just a sharp crook. Willing to spend a half million dollars for some information from a rat's brain.

And good old solid Paul Randall was screwing Alicia. What was it he told me when I first met him? Something about Dettman being married to a gorgeous, sweet woman. He probably got the information on Dettman cheating at cards from gorgeous, sweet Alicia.

And what was Dettman calling me a blackmailer for? I may have cheated him at cards and pilfered his papers, but blackmail?

The most interesting thing of all on the cassette was that call to Janet Drew. With her sick sister in Los Angeles. Janet was coming home tomorrow. I bet she was anxious to get back. Not for Dettman's charms, but to crawl under the bed and see what was on her tape recorder. At first I thought good old Ronnie had set the bugs to catch Janet in the sack with someone. But no, it had to be Janet Drew. Dettman wouldn't have let his conversation to Tokyo stay on the tape. And he wouldn't put the recorder in one of her Gucci shoe boxes under the bed. The likelihood of her finding it while looking for the right pair of shoes was too high. No, if it was Dettman, he'd have found a much better place to hide the recorder. But *Janet* didn't have to worry about *Dettman* looking into the boxes. I wondered where she had learned to bug a phone. And I wondered what she was doing with the information she got, and to whom she was selling it.

136

22

The San Francisco Airport is sort of the Winchester Mystery House of airports. The damn thing has been under construction for twenty-plus years, and it is nowhere near to being completed. It's sort of a full-employment project for the lucky building contractors who get their fingers in the contract pie.

I left the Ford in a spot marked "Airport Police Vehicles Only," near the central terminal, and wandered through barricades, potholes, over leaking hoses hooked up to hydrants, and across warped plywood boards covering God knows what to the North Terminal, which had been completed a couple of years ago and, which for some reason they hadn't started to knock down and remodel yet.

United Airline's flight number 34 was due to arrive at gate 87 from Los Angeles at 12:06, according to the flight schedule blinking on the screen above the entrance to concourse F.

137

It was only 11:30, so I bought a stale croissant and a cup of coffee and wandered down toward gate 87. I wanted to be in a position to see Janet Drew when she got off the plane.

The plane was on time, and I had no trouble spotting Drew. She was one of the first ones off. She was wearing a white skirt and matching jacket, the shoulders of which were right in the current style. A year from now it would look as if it was twenty years out of fashion. But then, she wouldn't think of wearing it a year from now. She wore red gloves, red shoes, and a round red hat with a bow in the back. Her purse was red too. In a word, she looked "expensive."

She walked with the grace of a model, long legs moving straight ahead, shoulders back, head up. She got a lot of stares, but ignored them in a casual sort of way. She was used to being stared at.

I followed her down to the lower level, where even people dressed like Janet Drew were forced to wait for their luggage.

I had planned to wait until she got her baggage, then tap her on the shoulder and ask if she wanted to buy a cassette tape. I never got the chance. While the baggage carousel was whirling around, spitting up suitcases, a familiar face came up and greeted Janet Drew warmly. Alicia Dettman put her arms around Drew, stood on her toes, and kissed Drew lightly on the cheek. Alicia was wearing faded denim pants and a light-blue tank top. She had on another pair of oversized sunglasses. They acted like two girls who hadn't seen each other since their last college reunion, all chatty and kissy.

Drew broke up the conversation long enough to pick

up two bags, both with the Gucci trademark stamped all over them. A porter took the bags and escorted the ladies outside, where Alicia's little Alfa-Romeo, with the top up, was parked against the curb. The porter managed to get one bag in the car's trunk, the other went in the backseat.

I started running back to where the Ford was parked. By the time I got back to the North Terminal, the Alfa was gone. I avoided a couple of collisions with a bus and a cab and made my way to the freeway headed north. The road construction saved me. Traffic had come to a snarly standstill and I spotted Alicia's sports car some twenty or so car lengths ahead of me. She didn't stay on the freeway long, turning off at South San Francisco. I followed her as she pulled into a Travelodge Motel. It was an old two-story affair spread out around a neglected swimming pool and an International House of Pancakes restaurant. The little red car scooted around the side of the motel. I got there just in time to see the two girls enter room 216.

I have gotten used to living in a somewhat confused state, but this really had my brain doing somersaults. What the hell were Alicia and Janet Drew doing in a motel room? Of course my dirty mind was racing through all kinds of possibilities. There are dozens of sleazy listening devices that can pick up conversations in motel rooms. Unfortunately, I didn't have one of the damn things with me. When I walked by the room, all I could hear was what sounded like the television set pouring out one of the afternoon soaps.

There were hardly any cars parked in front of the slots of the other rooms. Two cleaning women were pushing laundry bags from room to room. There was a good chance they'd spot me if I tried breaking into the room next to Alicia and Janet Drew. I could rent a room next to them, but without some kind of a listening device, I wouldn't learn much. They were in there for almost an hour and a half. When they finally came out they stood beside Alicia's car chatting merrily away. A cab pulled up, and the cabbie took the luggage from the Alfa, put it in his trunk; Janet Drew got in and they took off.

Alicia went back inside the room for a few minutes, then came out. She didn't have any luggage, but the oversized purse hanging around her shoulder looked as if it could hold enough clothes to fill up several dresser drawers.

She jumped into her convertible and took off, and I followed her back onto the freeway. She drove into San Francisco, taking the Broadway off ramp, and it looked as if she was headed toward her home. About a block before she got to the house I pulled up behind her, beeped the horn and waved, gesturing to her to pull over.

"That's really an ugly car," she said when I rested one hand on the roof of the Alfa and leaned down to talk to her.

"You should have seen my old one. Much worse. I was just going to drive by and see if you were home. I tried to call you earlier. Where were you?"

"Meeting a friend," she said, looking at the slim gold watch on her wrist. Her speech was slurred. "I hate to hurry off, Nick, but I've got to get home."

"We've got to talk, Alicia."

She put a hand on my arm and rubbed it gently. "I want to see you. We're good for each other, aren't we? But I've really got to go now."

She put the little car in gear and raced the engine.

140

"I found out something that may really help you get what you want from your husband."

She pushed her sunglasses against the bridge of her nose and peered up at me. "What have you found out, Nick?"

"Ron's got a steady girlfriend. He's paying the rent for her in a snazzy Russian Hill apartment. Sees her almost every day." I paused for what I thought would be great dramatic effect. "Remember me mentioning the name Janet Drew to you, the night you brought dinner to my place?"

Alicia threw her head back and laughed. "Oh, Ron and his women. I'm afraid I'll need more than that."

"And the name Janet Drew doesn't mean anything to you?" I asked. "She's a tall brunette. Very beautiful. Maybe twenty-five years of age. Looks like a model. Dresses very well."

She revved the car's motor again. "She sounds like she came off the assembly line. Ron always went for the tall brunettes. I really do have to go. Thanks for helping, Nick. I'll be in touch."

She waved a tan arm out the window as the little car squealed away from the curb.

23

Now what? I muttered to myself as I walked back to the
Ford. Why the hell didn't you tell her you saw her at the
airport? Why not confront her? I don't know, I answered
myself. It would have been a boring conversation if there
had been another person present, but with just me there,
it was more than I could handle. When I first went into
the police department, I worked under a wise old Irish
sergeant. When things became a bit too confusing, he'd
say, "That's a two-finger problem." If the shit had really
hit the fan, he'd say, "That's a three-finger problem."
The fingers came into use by holding them side by side at
the bottom of an empty glass, and then pouring bourbon
into the glass until it reached the top of the fingers.

There used to be a lot of "cops bars" in the city, but
not anymore. Now, most of the cops live in Marin County
or down the peninsula, so after they get off work they get
out of town as soon as possible. One of the few survivors is
Scully's, a watering hole on Judah Street, out in the foggy

trenches of the Sunset District. The owner is an ex-cop who took over the place when he left the department with a disability pension after being shot chasing a bank robber. The walls were covered with pictures of old policemen, on and off duty, in various shades of sobriety. The jukebox didn't have a song on it that was recorded after 1965.

"I've got a three-finger problem."

"Don't we all, pal," said Scully himself, a big, tall man with an immaculately groomed mustache that matched the silver color of his thick hair.

He poured me a Jack Daniels over. We did some shoptalk, played liar's dice, and he kept pouring. After about an hour of that I went and used the phone outside the men's room and called Janet Drew's number.

She sounded upset when she answered. I did the old fingers-on-the-throat routine again. "What's the matter, Janet? Didn't you get a nap at the Travelodge in South San Francisco?"

"What . . . who is this?"

"Have you looked under your bed yet? The Gucci shoe box. The tape's gone, Janet. I've got it."

Her voice had an edge of panic in it now. "Who is this? Please. What do you want?"

"Just some answers. Then you can have the tape back."

"I don't know what you mean—"

"Yes, you do. I know you've got a date with Ron tonight. Before he goes away on his trip. All that was on the tape. And a lot more."

"I just don't know what you're talking about. Just how—"

143

"You know. You can either meet with me, or I can talk to Ron about all this. Or maybe Inspector Tehaney would like to know about you and Alicia Dettman being such bosom pals."

Her voice regained some of its composure. "I assume you have something in mind, unless you're the type who gets his kicks making people squirm on the phone. When can we meet and discuss this rationally?"

Rationally. I liked that. "Tonight's out. I wouldn't want you breaking Ron's heart. I'll call you tomorrow morning." I remembered the line she'd given Dettman on the phone last night. "Sleep warm."

I went back to the bar and got into a three-man dice game. It was a little after five when Bob Tehaney walked in. I figured he would, since he lived only about three blocks away.

I bought him a drink.

"Anything new on the Price or Denko case, Bob?"

"No. I did catch Dettman out at the golf course. He didn't say much. Of course nobody seems to say much on this case. Including you. George Melleck is getting a little edgy. I wouldn't be surprised if you get a call from him. Seems that Dettman thinks you cheated him out of some money in a card game. Seems that—"

We were interrupted by his beeper going off.

"Goddamn things," he said angrily as he went to use the phone.

He was gone a good ten minutes. When he came back he looked grim.

"When was the last time you saw Maya Price?"

"Yesterday afternoon. Why?"

"That was the Belvedere Police Department. She's dead. Want to go for a ride?"

144

There was a marked police car blocking the driveway entrance to the Price house. Tehaney stopped to talk to the officer, and he waved us through.

Maya's maroon Aston Martin was parked in front of the garage. Another uniformed cop was at the front door. Tehaney showed his credentials again.

"I spoke to a Lieutenant Maklin on the phone. Is he here?" Tehaney asked.

A heavyset man with drooping shoulders came to the door. "I'm Maklin," he said. He was mostly bald, and there were some bumps on the top of his scalp that looked like the results of a hair transplant that didn't work. He wore a well-cut dark blue suit, a blue oxford shirt with a button-down collar and the collar fluffed just right. His tie was of heavy silk, in a shade of blue just about in between those of the suit and shirt. His loafers were highly polished. He looked too well-dressed to be a cop.

"The victim's upstairs, Inspector, in her bedroom. No sign of forced entry or evidence of any articles having been stolen. Of course, we'll have to get a full inventory of the premises. There are numerous items that are obviously quite valuable. We've checked with the neighbors. None have reported any unusual incidents, or any undesirable people in the area lately."

God, did he have to talk like that? Especially to another cop?

Tehaney frowned but handled it low-key. "It's your ball park, Lieutenant Maklin. Thanks for calling me."

Maklin waved an arm, inviting us into the house. He looked like a butler greeting guests at a cocktail party.

"This way," he said, and we padded up thickly carpeted stairs to the second floor. Some lab people were still in the bedroom dusting for prints. It was an elegant room,

145

with a silver-leaf ceiling. There was a brass-bonded mahogany armoire against one wall, a fireplace surrounded by glazed Moroccan tiles against the other. The windows were hung with delicate white curtains.

Maya Price's tiny body lay in the middle of a four-poster bed, covered with a white satin bedspread. Her eyes were closed and her mouth was open. Dried blood had hardened inside the mouth. Her right hand was lying behind her head in an awkward position. You could just make out the pearl handle of a pistol at the bottom of her hand.

"The coroner was held up because of a traffic accident up in Novato," Maklin said. "He should be here any minute."

"Who found her?" asked Tehaney.

"The cook. She comes in around two o'clock. Cleans up downstairs, gets dinner going. She saw Mrs. Price's car, so she thought she was home. Thought she was taking a nap. Came up to wake her, see just how many there were going to be for dinner. She estimates that she was here for a good two hours before coming to the bedroom and finding the victim."

Tehaney reached for a cigarette. Maklin gave him a frown. "I don't think it's wise to smoke, Inspector. Not until the lab men are through, at any rate."

Tehaney lit his cigarette and blew smoke at the ceiling. "Don't worry, Lieutenant. I won't drop any ashes on the carpet. So what do you think?"

Maklin folded his arms across his chest. "Well, of course we won't be able to formalize an opinion until the coroner, the laboratory, and our crisis team have completed their reports, but it certainly appears to be a sui-

146

cide." He unfolded his arms and smiled. "Grieving widow, you know how those things are." He looked around the room and shook his head. "Certainly a waste. The Prices were well respected in the community. A terrible waste."

"I've got two questions," I said.

Maklin turned his attention to me and raised an eyebrow. "Yes."

"Did she leave a note?"

"We haven't turned up one yet, sir."

He waited a moment, then said, "Your other question?"

"What the fuck is a crisis team?"

24

The drive back to San Francisco was not a pleasant one. I'd met Allen Price just once and really had no reason to like or dislike the man. There was nothing that I had done that could in any way be responsible for his death.

Ray Denko was a loser; sooner or later someone was going to kill him, and outside of the fact that I had been set up as a mugging victim for him, again, I really couldn't see how anything I had done was connected with his death.

But Maya Price was different. We had met—what?—twice, for a total of maybe half an hour. She was beautiful, intelligent, not exactly the most honest person I'd come across in the past few years, but in today's society, she would seem to pass for a pretty decent citizen. And I had played it cute, recorded our first meeting, and the tape was stolen. I tried to remember what she had told me that day. She told me that she knew I had swiped that set of documents from Dettman and returned them to him for the fourteen thousand dollars. Actually, I think her exact words were that I sold them to him for the fourteen grand. She claimed that Dettman had told her husband about the theft. That he was his attorney and "told him everything."

From what I knew of Dettman, he wouldn't tell his dentist which tooth hurt unless he had to. And why blab all that to Price? Paul Randall told me that Price was a specialist who handled real estate deals exclusively. A man like Dettman would have a half dozen attorneys, all specialists. Would he tell Price something like that? And if he didn't tell Price, who would? Janet Drew's name jumped to the head of the list.

Tehaney used the car's lighter to light a cigarette. I told him about the tape I'd made when I first met Maya Price.

"You think the tape was the reason they busted into your place?"

"No way they could have known about it, Bob. But they did find it. It might give them a motive for killing her. They'd know that her husband told her he was getting some highly classified documents that were worth a great deal of money. They'd know that she had other buyers for them."

Tehaney's face was a mere silhouette in the dashboard lighting. "Doesn't sound like much of a motive for killing her. And we don't know that she was murdered yet."

"When I saw her yesterday she didn't look like she was in any mood to commit suicide. Murder maybe, if she could find out who killed her husband."

"What if *she* killed him?" he asked.

"Why? What's the motive?"

He tapped some ashes toward the ashtray. He missed. "Who knows? She could have all kinds of motives. He was fooling around. He was going to leave her. He was keeping this big business deal to himself."

"When you interviewed her, did she have an alibi?"

He shook his head. "At home. Alone."

"There were two bottles of Dom Perignon in the trunk of Price's Jaguar. Did you ever trace them back to the liquor store?"

"Yeah. No problem there. The receipt was in the bag."

"You talk to the people at the store?"

"Yeah."

"Did he buy the wine chilled?"

Tehaney sighed, rolled down the window and flipped out his cigarette butt. "It was chilled. I know what you mean. Guy like Price isn't likely to buy chilled champagne in San Francisco, meet someone for a deal, then drive across the Bay to Belvedere to celebrate with his wife."

"So maybe the wine was for whoever was supposed to be bringing the documents."

"Maybe. Maybe he was just going to go over to some girlfriend's house after he got the documents. Who the hell knows? Shit," he said, reaching for another cigarette. "I ain't got enough troubles here, that asshole Maklin has to call me over to Belvedere. Maya Price is his problem. Let him handle it."

"Him and his crisis team."

Tehaney dropped me back at Scully's. Neither of us felt like having a drink, so I drove home.

"One of my mother's favorite sayings was, "When in doubt, eat." So I followed her advice. I took some gnocchi, pronounced nyok-kee, little potato-shaped dumplings in veal sauce that Mrs. Damonte had given me a few weeks back, out of the freezer, and made a small Caesar's salad. I had just started eating the salad when the doorbell rang. I opened it, half expecting to see Alicia Dettman with another care package from her caterer. Instead I saw the imposing figure of J. J. Murphy, Private Investigator.

He was rocking back and forth on his heels. "Good evening, Mr. Polo. My name is J. J. Murphy. I wonder if I might have a minute of your time."

"Sure, come on in, J. J. Had dinner yet?"

"I'm not interrupting your dinner, am I? If you have company, I can come back another time."

"No, no. Just me and some leftovers."

"That's all I wanted to know, asshole," he said, pulling out a revolver from under his raincoat.

"Murphy, grow up, will you. I'm tired, I'm hungry. I just left a police inspector and a dead body. I'm in no mood for fucking around with guns."

He jabbed the barrel into my stomach, which, I had to admit, certainly changed my mood in a hurry.

He got so close I could smell his breath. Either his dentist wasn't doing much of a job, or he'd missed his last few cleanings.

"Listen, punk," he said. "You've been making a pest of yourself. You did time once already. Didn't that teach you anything?"

"Yes. It taught me I should have used the same lawyer you did when the grand jury was chasing after you in

151

Los Angeles. Put the gun away, J. J. You're too old and too fat for the rough stuff."

He pulled the barrel back a few inches. "Who got killed?"

"Huh?"

"You said that you just left a police inspector and a dead body, hotshot. Whose body?"

"I'll tell you over salad. Come on into the kitchen."

Murphy followed me down the hallway, gun in his right hand, over the open palm of his left hand. He swiveled the gun around to the left and right as he entered the kitchen, just as they teach you to do at the police pistol ranges.

"Put that thing away before it goes off, Murphy. You probably haven't fired a gun in twenty years. If you're trying to impress me, you're not making it."

I started on my salad. He hooked a chair with his foot, turned it around so that he was sitting with his arms hanging over the chair's back, the gun still dangling from one hand.

"What did Dettman want you to do? Just scare me, or was there something he wanted to tell me?"

"Mr. Dettman has been pretty patient with you, Polo. But his patience is getting thin."

"J. J., if he sent you over here to scare me, he's not getting his money's worth." I stood up and went over to the oven and took out the gnocchi.

Murphy inhaled deeply and asked, "What's that?"

I told him. "Plates are in the cupboard. Silverware in that drawer. Though I guess you already know that."

He put his gun in its holster, took off his raincoat, and got the plate and silverware. "What kind of crack was that?" he said, helping himself to a large portion of the gnocchi.

"My place was broken into a few days ago. I figure it was Dettman's idea. I figure he'd have you do it."

"You kidding," he said, wiping sauce from his lips with the back of his hand. "Breaking and entering? Me?"

"Maybe you didn't do it yourself, but you hired someone. Ray Denko, probably."

"Denko? Never heard of him. I run a legitimate business, pal. No funny stuff."

"Bullshit. You do whatever your best client tells you to do, J. J. And Dettman is your best client. He points, you go."

"Damn, these things are good. Mind if I have a few more?" He took most of what was left in the pan. "Dettman wouldn't do anything stupid like have your place tossed."

"He's cheating on you, J. J. He hired a guy named Denko to beat me up. Denko's dead now. Murdered. Dettman can be a dangerous man to work for. First Allen Price, his attorney; then Denko, his strong-arm boy; now Maya Price. All dead. Tell me, was it you that followed his wife, got the pictures and the tapes? Or was he using someone else for that too?"

Murphy dropped his fork on his plate. "You asshole. That was you in the parking lot, wasn't it?" His hand started straying toward his gun.

"Don't try it, J. J. You'll end up ruining another pair of pants."

He stood up and I got up with him, staying close in case he tried for the gun. I shepherded him to the front door.

"Tell Mr. Dettman that I appreciate him going through the expense of sending you personally. And tell him I hope he has a smooth trip to Japan."

J. J.'s head snapped around. "How the hell did you know about that?"

"Tell him I know a lot more about him than he thinks I do. And be careful walking back to your car. A man could get mugged in this neighborhood."

25

The phone started ringing around eight-thirty in the morning. Clients, just when I didn't need them. But they were steady clients. An insurance company that handled small aircraft claims was in a hurry to find seven people for an upcoming trial. The accident had taken place almost six years ago. The witnesses had naturally moved around since then. They supplied me with dates of birth and social security numbers, so I put the mighty IBM to work. While I was doing that, an attorney called. He needed photographs of an accident site in San Mateo. And he needed them this afternoon.

It was almost ten-thirty by the time I finished playing with the IBM. I had told Janet Drew that I would call her at ten. What the hell, it was good to let her sweat a little bit.

No answer. Apparently sweating wasn't in her vocabulary. I drove down to San Mateo, photographed the site, dropped the film off at a one-hour developing shop, and had lunch while I waited for the pictures. I called Drew's number five times during lunch. Still no answer. I delivered the pictures to the client and went back to my flat. Still no answer at Drew's place, and no calls for me on my answering machine.

The computer had come through with enough information for me to run down the seven witnesses. I was on the phone to Los Angeles, Salem, Oregon, and Norman, Oklahoma, talking to police departments, libraries, county recorders, and voter registrars, but I got firm addresses for all seven of the witnesses.

The client was happy, and I felt as if I had done a full day's work. I wondered what the hell Janet Drew was up to. The way people were dying in this case made me nervous.

I drove up to her apartment building. The tall, skinny guy who had let me in when I swiped the cassette was on duty.

"Hi, Officer, how are you today? We haven't had any more problems, sir. None at all."

"I've been trying to get ahold of Janet Drew all day. There's been no answer. I'm a little worried."

"Let me check for you, sir."

He went into his little office and used the phone. He came out minutes later shaking his head. "No answer. I just came on duty about half an hour ago, and I haven't seen her."

I extended a hand. "Better give me the key. I'll check it out. This is probably a busy time for you; you don't want to leave your post."

He didn't hesitate. Not even for a second. A true believer in law and order. Probably had bumper stickers

156

proclaiming "Support Your Local Police" plastered all over his car. Probably watched *Dragnet* reruns. Probably stopped on the yellow at traffic signals. I felt rotten for deceiving him.

I pounded on the door to Drew's apartment before going in, wondering if maybe it would have been a better idea to bring the security guard with me. I'd have a lot more explaining to do if Janet Drew was lying in there with her hand wrapped around a pearl-handled pistol and a bloody hole in her head.

She wasn't there. No one was. And her closets were almost empty of clothes. There were a few dresses left, hanging limply on satin-covered hangers, a few lying on the ground, and a couple of Dettman's suits. The bed was covered with mismatched pieces of lingerie; the bureau drawers were open and empty. There wasn't a suitcase in sight. I bent down and looked under the bed. The Gucci box with the cassette recorder was gone too.

I went to the kitchen and helped myself to some of Drew's Scotch. At least she had left some liquor. Where the hell are you? Janet. In Japan with Dettman? No. Not even a fashion model would pack all her clothes. So where?

I tossed down the rest of the Scotch and went back downstairs.

"Any problems?" the security guard asked when I tossed him the key.

"No. What's your name?"

"Muniz. Larry Muniz."

"Larry, who was working when you came on duty?"

"Joey Hill."

"What hours did he work?"

"From eight in the morning till four in the afternoon, when I relieved him."

"Hill, is he a big guy, ex-Chicago cop?"

"Nah. That was Gene Gallagher. Big Gene. He's why everything is screwed up around here. He quit. That's why we've got to pull a double shift now every other day."

"Quit, huh?"

"Yeah. Just called in the other morning and said he was through." He shook a hand as if it was suddenly hot and he was trying to cool it off. "Let me tell you, management wasn't happy about that at all."

"Can you call this guy that worked today . . ."

"Joey Hill?"

"Yes. Call him and see if he knows anything about Janet Drew moving out today."

I paced nervously outside while Mr. Muniz called Hill. I could hear his side of the conversation.

"Yea, that's right, Drew. The good-looking broad in 1401."

He bobbed his head several times. "Yea, yea, okay."

He put his hand over the receiver and turned to me. "Hill says that she left in a cab with about six pieces of luggage around nine-thirty this morning."

"Ask him if Ronald Dettman was with her."

He went back to the phone.

"No, but he says Dettman had driven off when he came on duty. A little before eight."

"Did he hear her tell the cabdriver where she was going?"

He relayed the question.

"Nope. It was a yellow cab. He didn't get the number."

"Okay. Thanks."

I started for my car, then light bulbs began popping in my head. I went back to the little office. "Tell me more about this Gene Gallagher."

"Nice guy. Ex-cop. Man, he could really tell you some stories."

"How long did he work here?"

"A couple of months."

"You know where he lives?"

He hesitated a moment. "Yea, sure." There was a small, clear-plastic filing box on the corner of the desk. He went through the alphabetized indexes until he came to *G*, and pulled out a lined three-by-five card. The name Gene Gallagher, with an address and phone number of 649 Castillo Way, Pacifica, 555-4723, was printed in neat block letters.

"What you want to talk to Big Gene about, Officer?"

"How much an hour do you make, Mr. Muniz?"

"Six-fifty."

An ex-Chicago cop. A big, sharp ex-Chicago cop, working for six-fifty an hour. Why the hell didn't I think of him before?

The security guard was shouting something at me, but my mind was a million miles away. Or at least a couple of thousand miles away.

I went back to the flat, called telephone information, and got the number for the Chicago Police Department. I asked for the night-shift captain. His name was Mahoney.

"Captain Mahoney, this is Inspector Taylor, San Francisco Police Department. Sorry to trouble you, but one of your ex-boys is in a little shit out here and I'm just trying to find out what kind of a guy he is."

159

"What kind of shit?" he asked in a bottom-of-the barrel voice.

"Got in a fight at a bar. Picked the wrong guy. The mayor's nephew. Between you and me, the guy's a real asshole, and I'd like to squash the whole thing, but I'm not going to put my neck in the wringer for just anyone. The ex-Chicago cop is a guy named Gene Gallagher. Do you know him?"

There was a long pause. "Gallagher? About fifty. Fat guy, lost most of his hair?"

"No, Captain. He's a big man. Gray hair with the texture of a Brillo pad."

"What'd you say your name was?"

"Taylor, Inspector Ron Taylor. Badge number 535. I can give you a number and you can call back and verify if you want, but you'll have to do it fast. I've got to move on this, and to tell you the truth, if Gallagher wasn't an ex-cop, I'd have busted him right away. So what'll it be?"

That long pause again. "Okay. I know Gallagher. What was the fight about? A broad?"

"Right."

"Shit, the man worked vice back here for seven years, ran into enough pussy to float a battleship, still he was always getting in shit with the broads. What's he doing in Frisco?"

"I don't know."

"Last I heard he was working for one of the casinos, or some manufacturing plant in Vegas. Do what you can for him, Taylor. He's kind of an asshole, and he was in a little shit when he left here, but he's one of us."

"Thanks, Captain. I'll do what I can."

26

I called the number for Gallagher's place in Pacifica. I let it ring fifteen times. Then I lowered a finger, breaking the connection, and dialed the number at the police department for the homicide detail. No answer there, either. I could call the police general information number, or even 911, and get ahold of the homicide inspector on call. And tell him what? That I thought that a flashy-looking brunette and a big ex-Chicago cop were leaving town in a hurry, and that I thought that they were responsible for three murders? That I thought the police should put out an all-points bulletin for them right away? Not a bad idea, except that they might ask me what I had in the way of evidence to connect these people to the killings. And what did I have? Nothing really. The cassette tape of Dettman's voice, which proved nothing. Drew and Gallagher could deny knowing anything about it. And the police would ask some embarrassing questions about just how I'd come into possession of said tape. Besides, all-points bulletins sound impressive as hell in the movies and television, but all they are is a Teletype that goes out to district stations and outlying police departments. The Teletype clatters away on the station printer. A bored sergeant tears it off, posts a copy on the board, and reads it to the crew at the lineup. No one runs down the bus terminal, the train depot, or the airport and starts combing through the crowds on account of an all-points bulletin. However, if whoever is listed on the bulletin happens to break a speeding rule or run over a dog or a pedestrian, or drops his gun while going through the baggage check at the airport, then the all-points scores a few points.

I didn't think Gallagher was stupid enough to make a small mistake like that.

Pacifica is a little costal town just fifteen miles south of San Francisco. It's foggy and wet about ten months out of the year. The fog comes in early and stays late. Some days it never leaves. Housewives have been known to go a little crazy after being trapped in the cracker-box houses surrounded by the thick stuff day after day. You look out the window and it could be seven in the morning or seven at night. The view's always the same. Gray.

Castillo Way was a cul-de-sac a block or two from the Pacific Ocean. Each house had a minimum of two cars in front of the garage, chrome rusted, paint pitted. Each house except 649, which was what the realtors called "a junior ranch-style bungalow." Two small bedrooms, a combination living-dining room, a kitchen too small to fit a table in, and a two-car garage that actually might be able to accommodate two cars—if you stacked one on top of the other. The house had been painted brown and white when it was new. The brown had faded to a chalky beige and the white was dark and moldy in spots.

The front lawn was a neglected mixture of weeds, gopher holes, and bare ground. The laminated wooden front door had peeled down to its plywood undercoating. The drapes were pulled back from the windows alongside the front door. I peered in. It looked dark and empty.

I took out the Magnum and pushed the button for the doorbell. I heard a light buzzing. I waited, then knocked lightly on the door. Knocking hard would have put my fist right through the damn thing. I tried the doorknob. It was locked. I put the Swiss Army knife to work and in seconds was inside. I snapped on the lights. The living room consisted of one flower-patterned couch and a Sony TV.

There were a card table and four metal folding chairs in the dining area. The kitchen had a stove and refrigerator. A glass coffeepot with some coffee still in it was on the stove. I touched it. Ice cold. The refrigerator had a carton of half-and-half and a wilted head of lettuce. The freezer was jammed with frozen TV dinners.

One bedroom had an exercise bike and a set of barbells. The other had a double bed, the sheets and blankets twisted together, half on the bed, half on the floor. I was getting tired of looking in other people's closets, but it was a hard habit to break. Gallagher's held nothing but a half dozen metal clothes hangers. His dresser drawers were empty. Bare. Not even a leftover sock.

I went back through the kitchen and out to the garage. There were a shiny new bright-red ten-speed bike and a few hand tools. That was it.

I spoke to the neighbor next door, an attractive woman in her forties with dark, bored eyes.

"Mr. Gallagher? I didn't see him today. Nice man. Keeps to himself."

"Did he ever have many visitors?"

Her eyes lost some of their boredom. "Why you asking?"

I showed her my badge. "Just routine."

She stepped out on the porch and closed the door behind her. "He's a policeman too; did you know that?"

"Yes, I know. Did you ever see him with a tall, very attractive brunette?"

"He told me she was his sister. An airline stewardess, who stayed over once in a while." She shrugged her shoulders. "It's none of my business either way."

"Did he own the house or rent it?"

"Rented it. He's only been there a couple of months. Like I say, he's a nice man. Keeps pretty much to himself."

I thanked her and went back to my car, taking a few deep breaths of the ocean air before I headed back home.

27

I met Bob Tehaney for lunch the following day and told him my theories. He nodded his head, lit cigarette after cigarette and took an occasional note as he picked his way through a crab Louis salad.

"I'd like to talk to this Gallagher guy," he said. "And I want to talk to Janet Drew again, but if they've taken off, I've got nothing I can really go after them with. Right now I haven't got one damn thing I can use to tie them to Allen Price or Denko. And Belvedere says that Maya Price is going to go down as a suicide."

"I know, Bob. But could you call Chicago? Find out a little more on Gallagher. And also run Drew? I'd like to know the connection between them. Just where they originally met."

Tehaney called me later that day. Gallagher had done the minimum time in the department. Took his pension and headed off for Las Vegas. He worked as a security consultant to the Las Vegas Convention Center.

Janet Drew went by the names Janet Carlysle, Janet Dunn, and Janet Davenport. On one of her arrests, Gallagher had been the booking officer.

I put a call in to Ronald Dettman at his office in Sunnyvale. "Ask him to call Mr. Polo, and tell him it's about his trip to Japan and the meeting between Mr. Mercer and Mr. Yamato."

Dettman called back almost immediately.

"What the fuck are you up to now, you bastard? How did you find out about my trip to Japan?"

"I don't think it's something we should talk about on the phone. You know my address. I'll be here waiting."

It took him slightly more than an hour. He was escorted up the stairs by J. J. Murphy.

"Mr. Murphy is welcome to come in and join us, Ron, but I think you'd prefer this to be private."

"Wait," Dettman told Murphy, much like a man would give an order to his dog.

"This better be good, Polo," Dettman said when I closed the door on Murphy.

"Come on in the kitchen. Sit down."

He eyed the room nervously while I poured two cups of coffee.

I held up a cassette tape. "This was taken from a Gucci shoe box under the bed at Janet Drew's apartment on Taylor Street." I slotted the cassette into a portable radio-tape machine and punched the "play" button.

Dettman's eyes never left mine as he listened to the tape. When it was over, he asked, "What the fuck do you want for it, Polo?"

"Nothing. It's yours. And it's the only copy."

"Bullshit. Guys like you always have an angle. What is it?"

"Tell me about Janet Drew."

"Cunt. No-good cunt."

"She made the tape, Dettman. She and a guy named Gallagher."

"Gallagher? Who the fuck is Gallagher?"

"One of your doormen. Big guy with gray hair."

"Doormen?"

"They put the recorder in the apartment. Recorded every one of your calls, every one of your conversations for the past few months. Where did you meet Janet Drew?"

Dettman's hands started to tremble, making a faint tattoo on the tabletop. "I met her in Vegas. At a computer software convention. She was working one of the booths for this outfit that manufactures networking software. Shit, I need a drink."

I gave him a heavy bourbon on the rocks.

"How long ago was this?" I asked after he had knocked down half of the drink.

"About a year ago. She was bright, knew which fork to use, and had a mouth like a vacuum cleaner. We started seeing each other, then I moved her out here and set her up in the apartment."

"Did you introduce her to your wife?"

His head snapped up and his eyes narrowed. "How do you know about that?"

"Tell me about it."

"Alicia was making noises about a divorce again. She does every so often. I'd love to get rid of the bitch, but right now isn't the time. For business reasons, I need her available."

"You mean in case of a takeover you'd need her votes."

"Nothing so simple as that. But she could screw

167

things up. Make things difficult. I wanted to make sure I had something on her."

"So you had Janet Drew get chummy with her."

He drained his glass and looked up at me with sad eyes. I went and brought him the bottle.

"I had her get chummy with Alicia. It's not hard to get chummy with Alicia if she's had enough to drink. Boys, girls, it doesn't matter to her."

"So Janet introduced Alicia to some studs, or maybe the two of them got together to play button-button, who's got the bellybutton. And you got it on tape. What goes around comes around, Dettman. That might be where Janet got the idea to bug the apartment.

Dettman frowned and swirled the whiskey around in his glass for a moment. "Jesus Christ. That rotten bitch." He breathed deeply, like an athlete under the gun. "Find her for me, Polo. Find Janet and I'll pay you twenty-five thousand dollars."

"Why?"

"Why? Why the hell do you think? She screwed me. May have cost me goddamned millions. Millions! No telling what she was doing with the information she picked up at the apartment. Jesus, how could I be so stupid?"

"Those papers I took from your desk. Were they lying around the apartment? Could she have made copies, or have copied the material down?"

"I . . . I guess so. I may have left them there in the afternoon. Taken a nap. I'm just not sure."

"I think she did have copies made. There isn't a copy machine in the apartment, but the manager's office would have one. And Gallagher would have access to the office. She could have passed them to him, had the copies made, and put the originals back in your briefcase, all in under half an hour."

I went to the stove and replenished my coffee cup. "I think she did just that. And I think she was selling the stuff to Al Price."

"Price? No way. Al wouldn't . . . shit, the bastard probably would have at that."

"Price was murdered when he went to pick up those documents. Then that goon you sent after me, Ray Denko, got himself killed. He must have found out something about the papers. Then Maya Price was killed. She knew about the papers too. And she had several customers who were interested in them."

Dettman reached into his coat and pulled out a checkbook. "I told you I never sent anyone after you, Polo. I don't know anything about any of the murders. That's not my style." He used a gold fountain pen, no ballpoints for Mr. Dettman, and wrote out a check. He handed it to me. Five thousand dollars, made out to Nick Polo. "Find her, Polo. Find her and the next check you see will be for twenty thousand dollars."

J. J. Murphy was waiting dutifully at the front door.

"You know that old lady living in the place below you?" he asked me.

"Yes. Why?"

"She must be crazy. Kept popping her head out the door looking at me. Last time she gave me the finger."

28

It took almost seven months. Every couple of weeks I'd take Gallagher's and Drew's names and social security numbers and feed them into as many data-base programs as available to the mighty IBM.

In the end, none of that did any good, but there was a man down in Los Angeles, a retired bank executive who advertised himself as a "financial analyst." He had a computer that was somehow hooked into a data base used by the interstate banks, and the stuff he could pull out of that machine was truly amazing. Illegal as hell, but amazing.

I met the guy once. He was in his late sixties, short, at least a hundred pounds overweight. Sat in his beautiful estate, taking calls from guys like me who don't have the connections he does, and made a fortune. He never left his house. Just answered his phone and sat in front of his computer. A regular Nero Wolfe, and he didn't even need an Archie to go out and beat the pavements for him.

Driver's licenses; easy to forge, even easier to get a real one under a false name. Just mosey across the border to Oregon, tell the DMV people there that you just moved into the state and need a license. They are happy to give you one, right then and there, thanks to the Polaroid camera. Then you come back to California, get a new license under the phony name you gave in Oregon. No problem.

Anyone who's read a few spy novels knows the technique to get a passport. You go to a cemetery, find the tombstone of an infant or young child born around the same time you were, go to the county clerk, get a copy of the deceased's birth certificate, and use it to apply for the passport. The problem with this process is that this is so easy and so popular, you run the risk of someone else having used the same name, and now several states have smartened up and are stamping "Deceased" on the birth certificates.

Ah, but the social security number, that's different. It is the universal identifier. If you use someone else's, sooner or later the great computer in the sky is going to get you.

You can use a number that hasn't been issued yet, and that may work for a couple of years. But once you start using that number to open bank accounts, checking accounts, anything to do with money, you become vulnerable.

And Janet Drew and Gene Gallagher had a lot of money. They had to do something with it. They were shrewd enough to sell Dettman's plans for top dollar. Cash may be king, but when you're sitting on bags of it and it's not making any interest, you've got to put it to

171

work for you to make more money, or pretty soon you'll run out of it.

The feds have made it tough on anyone by extending the Bank Secrecy Act so that even gambling casinos must report all cash transactions involving more than ten thousand dollars.

So you've got all this money, and you want to buy a nice Mercedes, or BMW. Can't go in and give the dealer the fifty or sixty thousand he wants in cash, so what do you do? Buy a Datsun, Toyota, whatever, for nine thousand, go and turn it in, at a big loss, for a Ford or Chevy, add something under the ten-thousand-dollar cash figure, get that car, and trade it up again, along with some more cash. Confusing, no? Who said being rich was easy?

Gallagher had left a bank account in San Francisco with some nineteen thousand dollars in it. His retirement check from the Chicago Police Department was posted to the bank monthly. It was building up to a tidy nest egg. But he was too smart just to come into the bank and pick it up. Or have them transfer the money to another bank in his name.

Gallagher was sharp enough, and had enough connections, to be able to check to see just how interested the police were in him and Janet Drew. In fact, they were not very interested at all. There were no wants, no warrants, not even an official inquiry on record for either of them. Poor Maya Price was officially a suicide, and the Allen Price and Ray Denko murders were ancient history now. Unless Gallagher or Drew did something stupid or dropped in and sat on Inspector Tehaney's lap, they were home free.

So they got stupid. Or lazy. Or greedy. They didn't

figure that someone like me would be chasing after them. And if it hadn't been for the twenty thousand dollars offered by Ron Dettman, I wouldn't have.

Gallagher opened an account with a stockbroker in San Diego under his name and used his social security number. My "financial analyst" friend picked up the information and forwarded it to me.

Gallagher, or Drew, was playing the option markets in a pretty heavy way. The address the stockbroker's firm had for them was 3355 Rosencrans Street, number 1207, in San Diego.

I called Dettman.

"I think I've found Janet Drew."

"Christ, I almost forgot about you, Polo," Dettman said. "Where is she?"

"Possibly San Diego."

"Possibly?"

"Right. Gallagher is doing some banking down there. I've got an address. I'm not sure if it's good yet."

"And you think Janet is still with him?"

"If not, he'll know where she is."

"Okay. Go and talk to her. Don't bring the cops in on this. I want to meet with her."

"Don't bring in the cops? What about the little matter of a few murders?"

"I want to talk to her," he repeated. "It's important. I want to find out just who she was selling me out to. And for how much. And, most importantly, what she gave them."

"You mean, even if I do find her, you wouldn't press charges?"

"For what, smart guy? For running a recording ma-

173

chine on her own phone? I'm not aware that is a crime. Just find her. Let me know where she is. I want to see her."

"There's a small problem of money. I've spent most of the five thousand you advanced me to get this far."

"Now you're sounding more like the Polo I've grown to know and hate. Okay. I'll send you another five thousand. The rest of the deal still stands. You call me when you've got her, and you get fifteen thousand more. When are you going down to San Diego?"

"As soon as your check clears."

29

Number 3355 Rosencrans turned out to be one of those private postal-box places. It was located in the downtown area of San Diego, just a few blocks from the airport and across from a naval training center and seemed to do a big business with members of the armed services: marines, sailors, soldiers went in and out of the swinging doors every few minutes.

Now the real post office, the one the government claims it runs, isn't too bad. There are a couple of ways of getting the name and address used by the box renter, but the private outfits are a different story.

I went into the building and found box number 1207. It was no bigger, no smaller than any of the other boxes. The boxes were about the size that would accommodate a loaf of French bread and had solid metal fronts, so you couldn't see what was inside.

It was a warm day with just a slight breeze. I parked the rental Chevrolet sedan I'd picked up down the street, and sat and sweated with the car windows down until 7:00 P.M., when the box-rental place closed.

The art of surveillance requires two specific physical attributes: strong kidneys and a weak mind. I might have faked it with the mind, but you can't fool Mother Nature, so the next morning I was up bright and early and rented a Winnebago, with a nice little bathroom and stove, and parked it right in the lot adjacent to the private post office. The Winnebago was roomy and comfortable, but it was certainly going to stand out if I had to follow Gallagher or Drew in it, which meant I had to have the sedan close by, which meant parking tickets.

I went a whole day, from nine in the morning until seven in the evening, and there was no sign of Drew or Gallagher. The Chevy had picked up two parking tags.

I was back the next morning, armed with donuts and delicatessen sandwiches. It was almost eleven when a white Mercedes coupe purred into the parking lot, with Janet Drew behind the wheel.

I copied down the plate number and ran to the Chevrolet and got back just in time to see Drew stride toward the Mercedes. She was wearing white pants and a bright yellow tank top and got her allotted share of admiring glances from the milling servicemen.

I followed the Mercedes up Rosencrans onto highway 5; she went north for a few miles, past Mission Bay, took the off ramp marked "highway 74," then made a left toward Pacific Beach. I kept my eyes glued to her tail-lights, because this was all new country to me. If I lost her here, I'd have no idea just where she was going. She made another right, then a left, and finally drove under an arched stucco gateway proclaiming "El Dorado Con-

176

dominiums." The grass was nicely trimmed and flowering bougainvillea seemed to be everywhere. The condos were two-story adobe-style affairs. Drew parked in front of one numbered 327, waited for the garage door to open, and drove inside, the door closing after her with a discreet thud.

I drove by, made a U-turn, and went back and parked in a spot marked "Reserved for Visitors." A bright blue-and-white-striped awning lead to the condo rental offices.

A tall blond-haired man in his thirties with a deep tan greeted me. "Dick McKevitt," he said. "Can I help you?" He had a strong handshake.

"I'm contemplating moving to San Diego and I'm looking for a nice quiet area," I told him.

"Well, you've certainly come to the right place, Mr.——?"

"Dr. Ross."

The doctor bit always seemed to get them. His eyes glazed a bit as he realized he had a live one who could afford whatever rents they were asking.

"Are you thinking of leasing or buying, Doctor?"

"I'm not sure. Can you show what you have available?"

He could, and did. The condos were all nicely done, the interior walls almost a duplicate of the outside stucco, the ceilings beamed with tongue-and-groove planking.

He gave me the full tour, including the community swimming pool and exercise room.

"For two thousand a month, you can hardly beat it, Doctor."

"I like it. Do you have any brochures I can show my wife?"

He supplied me with half a pound or so of slick literature extolling the virtues of the El Dorado Condominiums.

"I think I have some friends staying with you now. The Gallaghers."

A frown creased his sunburned forehead. "Gallagher? I don't recognize that name."

"Maybe I'm wrong. Maybe it was Janet Drew. I thought she told my wife she'd moved down here."

He gave me a salesman's smile. "No. I don't recall that name either. Perhaps it was one of the older condos farther down the beach."

I looked at my watch. "I've got a little time to kill before I have to catch the plane back to San Francisco. Mind if I stroll along your beach?"

"Not at all, Doctor. That's one of the many benefits of living here. The units all have beach access and you're free to use it as often as you want." His voice deepened. "Of course we have excellent security, so you don't have to worry about any strangers wandering along the beach behind your unit. We're very careful about that."

"Yes, I'm sure you are," I said, thanking him again.

I left my coat jacket in the car, rolled up my sleeves, and wandered down to the beach. There was a pleasant breeze coming in off the Pacific. The waves lapped up lazily, leaving an edge of foam against the white sand. I walked close to the water, where the sand was hard-packed, and walked down past the condo Janet Drew had driven into. The draperies were drawn on both the ground and second floor.

I wandered back toward the car. Decision time. Either I made a move now, or left and called the cops, or called Dettman. The salesman would start wondering about Dr. Ross if I hung around much longer and he'd call on his security people to check me out.

I turned back to the beach and headed for the Drew condo, not really having any idea of just what the hell I was going to do when I got there.

There was a deck in the back of the unit, raised some five feet above the beach. Streaks of sunlight came through the deck planking, throwing zebralike shadows on the sand.

I could hear the sound of a radio coming from inside.

What I couldn't hear was the footsteps coming up from behind me. Suddenly something was poking me in the back.

"Couldn't keep your fucking nose out of it, huh, hotshot?"

I twisted my neck around halfway and saw the smiling face of Gene Gallagher glaring down at me.

"Walk. Around the back. Up those steps."

The glass patio doors slid open as we got near the back of the unit.

Janet Drew was waiting inside. When Gallagher closed the patio doors behind us, she walked over and slapped me with the back of her hand.

"You bastard," she snarled. "What the hell do you want now?"

I rubbed my chin. For a woman, she packed a good punch. I looked at Gallagher. No wonder I hadn't heard him come up behind me. He was barefooted, wearing a pair of khaki Bermuda shorts and a flower-patterned sport

179

shirt. His legs, arms, and face were a blotchy red color. He had the kind of skin that would never take a tan. A towel he had held in one hand dropped to the floor. I wasn't surprised that there had been a gun hidden under it—a long-barreled automatic.

"I saw you walking down the beach, Polo. How the hell did you find us?"

"That's not important. What is important—"

He smashed the gun barrel across my cheek. I could feel the blood spurt out.

"I'll decide what's important and what's not. How did you find us?"

"Your account with the stockbroker," I said, using the back of my hand to wipe some blood off my cheek.

"Who else knows you're here?"

"Dettman."

"Shit," Gallagher snarled. He turned to Janet Drew. "Pack. Quick. Just take what you need."

Janet Drew dropped down onto a canvas-back deck chair as if her legs had suddenly lost all their strength. "I'm sick and tired of packing and moving. Sick and tired of not being able to spend the money like you promised we would. We have to live like fucking hermits." She pounded her fist into her leg. "I'm just fucking sick of it all."

"Yeah, me too, baby. But this asshole doesn't leave us much of a choice."

"Dettman doesn't want to go to the cops. He just wants to talk to Janet," I said.

Gallagher walked over to me, shoved a brawny hand under my chin, and pushed my head into the wall. "Do you have any idea of how much money you've cost us,

180

asshole? We had a perfect setup with Dettman. Perfect, until you came along and fucked it up."

"What about Al Price?" I asked, straining to talk through the grip he had on my chin.

He wrenched his hand away. "What about him?"

"I thought he was the one that screwed things up. He and his wife Maya."

"You think too much, asshole." He turned to Janet Drew. "Pack, goddammit. Right now."

She stood up reluctantly. "I'm tired of it." Her eyes bored into me.

"What's the rush? I'm telling you, Dettman just wants to talk to Janet. Find out just what it was that she sold to his competitors. And who she sold it to."

"Sure, that's all he wants, but what about the cops?" asked Gallagher.

"You must have checked," I said. "There's nothing out on either of you. Nothing at all."

"Bullshit," Gallagher said. "You tell them where we are and they'll be all over us." He raised the gun up to my stomach. "I ought to belly-shoot you, you prick. But since we're both ex-cops, I'm going to be nice and just put a slug into your brain. Make it easy on you."

"Why kill me? Then you will be in shit. Dettman knows I'm here. I was just over there talking to the condo salesman, McKevitt. My car is parked in front of his office. Kill me and you're waving a red flag at the cops."

"Maybe he's right, Gene," Janet Drew said.

"He's bullshitting, is what he's doing. Trying to save his skin. You think Dettman is going to let you walk away from him after what you did? You think the cops are just going to forget about Price and his old lady? Use your fucking head for something besides giving head for once, stupid."

There was the sound of shouting coming from the beach.

"Check it out," Gallagher said nervously.

Janet Drew pulled the patio door draperies back and peeked out. "It's the people from next door, playing volleyball again."

"Shit. Okay, come over here." He went to a kitchen cabinet and took out another gun. This one was a revolver. He handed Drew the gun. "Keep it on this bastard. If he moves, pull the trigger. We'll worry about those assholes out back later."

He went to the refrigerator. "Where's the Seven-Up, damn it?"

"There's more in the garage."

"Keep that gun on him."

Gallagher went out a door in the back of the kitchen.

"Look, Janet. Don't let him kill me. I wasn't kidding about Dettman. He wants to talk. He'll even pay you to find out just which competitors you sold his information to. Right now, you're clean. There's no way to tie you to Al Price's murder, and Maya Price is an official suicide. Dettman won't press charges of any kind. You won't have to run anymore. He doesn't want to hurt you, he just wants to talk. He's not a bad guy."

"Not a bad guy! He's a miserable pervert who liked to play naughty games with bananas. He made me go after his own wife. He treated me like a whore."

Gallagher pounded back into the kitchen carrying a plastic liter-sized bottle of 7-Up.

"Ever see this trick, Polo?" he asked, unscrewing

182

the top of the bottle and dumping the contents into the sink. He walked over to a coffee table, picked up a box of Kleenex, and started stuffing tissues into the bottle. "A poor man's silencer." He laughed. "You're going to be the poor man."

He shoved the automatic's barrel into the bottle until it was up against the frame of the gun's trigger housing. "Get me some Scotch tape," he said to Drew.

She went over to the side of the room and up a flight of stairs. "Yeah, it's too bad you came along, Polo. I liked it here. This is real California. Good weather all the time. Racetrack up in Del Mar, or you can just travel a few miles down into Mexico. Horses, dog races, anything you want. And warm, man, real warm, none of that damn Frisco fog."

Janet came back and gave him the tape, which he used to wrap around the gun and plastic bottle.

"Got to make the seal real tight," he said, wrapping the tape until the roll was empty. "Only problem with this thing is they're not very accurate. You've got to be close. Real close."

He came within a couple of feet of me and pointed the contraption at my head. "Doesn't silence it completely, but it'll have to do."

"Listen, I—"

"Too late, Polo."

I felt my bowels loosening, my blood racing as I got ready to make a final, futile leap at Gallagher.

"Wait," Janet Drew said. "Let me do it."

"What? You do it? What for?" Gallagher asked, backing away a few feet.

"Because if it wasn't for him, we'd have been sitting

pretty—rich, real rich. He's the one that fucked everything up. Let me do it, Gene."

Gallagher laughed. "Never thought you were that popular, I bet, huh, Polo?"

He used both hands to pass the silenced weapon to her. "Make it quick, baby. We've got to get out of here."

Janet Drew took the gun, then said, "You killed Allen and Maya Price, didn't you?"

Gallagher managed to say something like "huh" or "wa" or "oh" before she pulled the trigger. He was right. The first slug wasn't completely silent, but it was only about a third as loud as the next four. Janet Drew put five bullets into his head.

She swiveled the gun back to me.

"You heard him, didn't you? He admitted killing Al and Maya Price. I set up the meeting with Al that night. I was going to take the copies of the papers, but Gallagher wouldn't let me go. He met Price. I didn't know he was going to kill him. He was just supposed to pick up the money." Her eyes glazed over. The words were rushing out of her mouth, each one louder than the last. "It was Gallagher who set up the bugs, and I didn't know anything about it. You'll testify to that, won't you?"

"Right," I mumbled through thick lips.

She took in a gulp of air, like a swimmer getting ready to dive to the bottom of the pool. "I saved your life, remember that, and remember what you promised. Dettman won't press any charges, and he's going to pay me for what I tell him about who Gallagher sold the information to, right?"

"Right, anything you say is right, Janet," I said as she dropped the gun with its shredded silencer to the floor.

30

It was past eight in the evening by the time the San Diego Police Department was satisfied enough with my statement to release me.

In between my talks with a half dozen different police officers, I called Dettman. He didn't seem overjoyed about the news, but said that he would fly right down to talk to me.

I didn't wait for him when I left police headquarters. I was tired, hungry, and burned out. There's something about being close enough to death to smell it that takes all the starch out of you. My motel was a typical Holiday Inn in the downtown area of the city. I went to my room for a shower, then headed to the motel's restaurant. I had two drinks and ordered their largest cut of prime rib. Both the drinks and the food seemed tasteless, though I couldn't blame it on the kitchen. Even one of Mrs. Damonte's special veal dishes would have probably tasted like cardboard to me right then.

My hands would start to shake all of a sudden and I needed both of them to handle the meal-ending cup of coffee.

While I had promised Janet Drew that anything she said was right, as soon as she dropped the gun and the cops showed up, I told them exactly what I thought. That Drew and Gallagher were into the Allen Price murder together, and that I wouldn't be surprised if Janet actually pulled the trigger. Price wouldn't have ordered those chilled bottles of champagne for Gallagher, and I have a feeling he wouldn't have just rolled down his window to talk to him while parked in a deserted area under the freeway in the dark of the night either. Maybe Janet didn't pull the trigger, but she was there that night.

Maya Price was another matter. The Belvedere Police Department still listed the case as a suicide.

The police had examined us separately, and at one point together. Janet Drew had stuck to her story; Gallagher had known her in Chicago. Had bumped into her accidentally when they were both working in Vegas, and, when she met up with Ronald Dettman, told her he would expose her past criminal career as a prostitute if she didn't help him bug her apartment to obtain confidential information on Dettman Industries. She said it was Gallagher who killed Allen Price. Price was going to pay them ten thousand dollars for the plans. From listening to Dettman's phone calls, they knew they were worth a lot more. She said that Gallagher was worried about me, so he broke into my flat, planted the bugs there, found the cassette recorder with the conversation between myself and Maya Price. That's what gave Gallagher the idea to see Maya, get the names of her contacts. Maya wouldn't

186

cooperate, so he killed her, making it look like a suicide. It had all been Gallagher's doing. All his fault. Janet seemed to have the ability to turn her tears on and off as easily as she worked the shower nozzle.

Her story was that after they left San Francisco, she and Gallagher went to Hawaii, then traveled around the states, finally settling in San Diego.

She claimed that Gallagher beat her, kept her in constant fear of her life, told her that he had told some of his friends about her, put a contract out on her, so if she ever turned him in, they'd kill her, and that's why she never contacted the police.

The San Diego cops seemed to believe her about as much as I did, but proving something different was going to be a task.

The most interesting thing that came up, or rather didn't come up, was Ray Denko. Drew claimed she never heard of the man. Unfortunately, that was the one part of her testimony that I did believe.

I went back to my room and tried to sleep. Dettman called at midnight. He had just gotten in and wanted to talk.

"Come over here now, Polo. Right now."

"Tomorrow morning, Dettman. I'm beat. It'll have to be tomorrow morning."

"Damn it, I want to talk to you now. We've got some problems. Big problems."

"Where are you?"

"The Coronado."

"See you for breakfast," I said, then hung up and left the receiver off the hook.

I didn't sleep much. I kept running everything

187

through my mind, then I'd doze, then wake up again. It was a long, confusing night.

I checked out of the motel by eight, turned in the Winnebago first, then the Chevy, then took a cab to the hotel to meet Dettman.

They say that the suites at the Hotel del Coronado have been occupied by everyone from the Duke and Duchess of Windsor to most of the U.S. Presidents and tons of so-called movie stars. It claims to have been the first hotel in the world with electric lights, and that Thomas Edison himself supervised the installation. I mean, we are talking history, class, and old money here. It's really a Victorian masterpiece, all white towers and cupolas, with a distinctive red lead-colored roof. They've filmed hundreds of movies there, including *Some Like It Hot,* with Marilyn Monroe.

Somehow Dettman didn't seem to fit in, but his suite was everything that a suite costing probably four hundred a night should be. He was sitting at a breakfast table covered with plates of bacon, ham, sausages, scrambled eggs, three or four kinds of muffins, and enough fruit to make up one of Carmen Miranda's hats.

Janet Drew was sitting across the table from him.

Dettman waved a hand. "Sit down, Polo. Have some coffee. Help yourself. We've already started."

"Already started what?" I asked, pouring myself a cup of coffee.

"Janet tells me she saved your life yesterday."

"Janet saved her own life yesterday too; didn't you, Janet?"

She was wearing a yellow-and-white polka-dot sundress held up by two thin spaghetti straps. Her hair was

188

done just right, makeup perfect. She looked as if she was waiting for the photographer from *Vogue* to call her down to the pool for a fashion session. Hell, for all I know, she was. She certainly seemed to know how to land on her feet.

"I think I'll leave. I'm sure you two gentlemen want to be alone."

She stood, giving me a steely glance as she passed by.

I stuck my tongue out at her, but she didn't even blink one of those perfectly mascaraed eyes.

"Have something to eat, Polo," Dettman said.

"No, thanks. But I will take a check for fifteen thousand dollars."

He leaned back in his chair and patted his lips with a linen napkin. "You really think you earned it?"

"Yes. Almost getting killed seems to be worth a lot of money to me."

"You can thank Janet for saving your ass. And you can thank me for being a good sport." He took a checkbook out of his jacket pocket. He spoke as he wrote. "As far as I'm concerned, you bungled the job. All you had to do was call me. I could have handled it from there."

"Handled it? You mean taken care of Gallagher?"

He tore off the check and handed it to me. The numbers were correct. Fifteen thousand dollars.

"This publicity isn't going to do me a lot of good, Polo. Not at all. But at least I pumped Janet, learned just who she was peddling my stuff to. You wouldn't believe what these bastards were paying for my research."

"I'd believe it. Remember, I had the tape of you

talking to your friend in Japan. You were going to pay him a half million, weren't you?"

Dettman picked up the coffeepot and filled both our cups. "It's tough out there, Polo. Tarzan wasn't kidding Jane. It is a jungle. You do what you have to do."

"What are you going to do about Janet Drew?"

He took a sip of the coffee, holding it in his mouth and swishing it around his teeth before he swallowed. "Nothing. I'm setting her up with a top-gun criminal attorney. That way I can keep an eye on just what she's going to be telling the cops. And he can make sure she gets what she really deserves. I got most of what I needed to know from her this morning."

"At a price again?"

"Everybody's got a price, Polo. Everyone. That's why you took that check."

"I'll give you a chance to get the fifteen thousand dollars back, Dettman. Just tell me where you met Ray Denko."

"Never met him, never heard of him."

"And you never sent him after me to get back that fourteen thousand I won from you in the poker game."

"You sound like a broken record, Polo. I keep telling you, I never sent anyone after you."

I drained my coffee and stood up. Dettman just looked at me, a satisfied smirk on his face.

"You know, Dettman, you're such an asshole that I really hate doing a favor for you. But it looks like I have to."

31

"I want to buy you a drink."

Alicia Dettman looked back at me with sleepy eyes.

"Oh, it's you," she said, putting a hand on her forehead as if to shade her eyes from the sun, even though it was dark out.

I hadn't seen Alicia in over half a year and time hadn't been kind to her. Her face was puffier, the crow's-feet deeper.

"I really can't, Nick, I'm expecting company, and Ron may be home at any time. You should have called."

"I insist, Alicia," I said, walking past her into the house. "Where's your purse?"

"Really, I can't just—"

"I've got a surprise for you, Alicia. A big surprise. And there's someone you just have to meet. Come on, it won't take long. Ron won't be back tonight. He's still in San Diego. Get your purse."

She protested again, and I followed her upstairs to

191

her bedroom. She was wearing a black-and-tan-plaid skirt and beige blouse.

"Just get a sweater," I told her. "We won't be long."

She reached for her purse and I grabbed it from her, weighing it in my hand before passing it over.

"What's come over you, Nick?" she asked as I took her out of the house and to my car.

Once in the car she started chatting away at a rapid pace, telling me that she had called me several times and tried getting ahold of me, and that she and Ron were getting along much better now.

I parked across from Ferrando's bar and turned the motor off.

"Remember this place, Alicia?"

"No. I never get to this part of town. Why did you bring me here?"

I got out and opened the door. "Denko used to work here. Didn't you ever meet here? Have a couple of drinks before you went to his place? I was trying to figure out just where you met him. Was it the track? Those pictures of you and Ron at the track, you must have spent a lot of time down there. You owned a few racehorses, didn't you?"

She climbed out of the car, took a step, then leaned back against the door.

"I don't want to go in there, Nick."

"Why not? You look like you need a drink."

I grabbed her wrist and pulled her across the street. The bar was crowded. It was Friday night. The start of a promising weekend for a lot of people.

The same guy who had been there the last time was behind the bar. He put two napkins down in front of us.

"Hey, *paisan*," he said. "Good to see you back. What'll it be?"

"Two vodkas over. That okay with you, Alicia?"

She nodded her head, her eyes looking down at the cocktail napkin.

The bartender brought the drinks and I introduced them. "Alicia, this is Mr. Ferrando. He owns the place. Ray Denko was his brother-in-law."

"Pleased to meet you, miss. You knew Ray?"

Alicia pulled her head up and looked at him. "No. I don't know who he was."

"Sure you do, Alicia. You probably never met Mr. Ferrando because he worked the day shift when Ray was here. But I bet a lot of the regulars remember you. Ray must have brought you in. He'd want to show you off, that's the kind of guy he was, right, Ferrando?"

The bartender used a towel to wipe the bar. "Yeah, Ray liked to show his ladies off, all right."

A man came and sat on the stool next to Alicia and she almost jumped off her seat when he bumped into her. She looked at him quickly, then turned away, picking up her drink.

The far end of the bar was crowded with a dozen or more men.

"Want to go down and see if any of Ray's friends are down there? I'll bet there're a few that will remember you, Alicia. A woman like you gets remembered in a bar like this."

She had a habit of running her tongue around her mouth, imparting a moist sheen to her lips. She did it now, then turned to me and said, "Why are you doing this to me, Nick? Why?"

193

"Why did you turn Ray Denko on me? It was you, Alicia. It had to be. You checked the envelope that night. Knew it was full of money. Where was Denko? In the house? Waiting outside? Where?"

She stared down into her glass as if it were a crystal ball. "He was outside. I knew about the money. Ron was furious about it. He knew your name was really Polo, but he was going to give you the money anyway, said it was worth it to know who his real friends were. He kept calling Paul Randall a bastard for taking you to the club."

"What did you need the money for?"

She sighed, then took a swallow of her drink. "I didn't really. But Ray did. He was losing a lot of money at the track. He kept pushing me for money. Cash. Ron never gave me much cash."

"Why were you so interested in giving cash to Denko?"

"He . . . he was going to do something for me."

"Something like kill your husband?"

Her voice lowered to a confessional whisper. "Yes. He said he would. But he wanted money. A lot of money."

"But he never really planned on killing Ron, did he?"

She stood up and walked over to a small table. I picked up her drink and carried it over to her.

"He never did plan on killing Ron for you, did he?" I repeated.

"After he got the money from you, he was mad. He thought it was going to be a lot more. He had it all planned out. He'd take the money, make you think that my husband had sent him, then, when he killed Ron,

194

you'd be a suspect." She ran a finger down her cheek, hard enough to leave a mark. "He came back after he got the money. He hit me, said that the money wasn't enough. That he'd need more. I knew then that he'd never go through with it. He was just all talk, like so many men. Just all talk."

"But you continued seeing him, didn't you?"

The bartender brought over two unasked-for drinks. I was beginning to wonder if he'd lost his touch.

Alicia stuck her finger in the drink and moved the ice cubes around. "I saw him a few more times."

"You saw him at his apartment. You drank with him, slept with him, then, when he was in the shower, you shot him. Probably with that gun your husband kept in his bedroom. Why, Alicia? Why the hell did you have to kill him?"

She crossed her arms over her chest and looked straight into my eyes. "Because he was like all of you. Use me, get tired of me, then pass me around. He wanted to bring one of his friends over to his run-down apartment. 'Have a three-way' was the charming way he put it. He was ready to turn me over to one of his buddies. He promised to kill Ron for me. He didn't have the guts, then he thought he could use me to pay off one of his gambling debts. That's why I did it."

"Is that why you got turned off on men? Is that why you started seeing Janet Drew?"

She picked up her drink and shook her head. "Janet's all right. That wonderful, sweet husband of mine put her up to meeting me. After a while she told me all about him. She was going to help me get rid of Ron. She hated him too. But she left. I guess she couldn't stand any more of him either."

"That man at the bar. The one that was sitting next to you. His name is Inspector Robert Tehaney of the San Francisco Police Department. He's going to have to talk to you, Alicia. You must have left prints all over Denko's apartment. He'll be able to find people who saw you and Denko together. He'll put all the pieces together."

She leaned across the table. "Why are you doing this to me? Is my husband paying you? No one in the whole world cares about Ray Denko. He's better off dead. So why are you doing this to me, damn it?" She leaned back, turned her head away and started to cry.

They were questions I really didn't have a good answer for. I went back to the bar and sat next to Tehaney.

"Ron Dettman kept a .38 revolver in his bedroom. I wouldn't be surprised if that was the gun she used on Denko."

"She admit she killed him?" asked Tehaney.

"Yes. She admitted it."

The legs of the stool scraped loudly against the linoleum as Tehaney stood up. He gave me a sour look, then went over to see Alicia. I watched them talking. Watched Tehaney take her by the elbow and escort her out the door.

The bartender put a drink in front of me.

"Don't you ever wait until you're asked, damn it?" I said in a voice so loud it surprised me.

He backed away, put both palms up and shrugged. "Hey, *paisan*. I've been in this business long enough, I don't have to ask. I can tell just by lookin' when a guy needs another drink. And buddy, you look like you really need it."

I couldn't argue with him.